Avenging Alex

Avenging Alex

Lewis Ericson

www.urbanbooks.net

Urban Books, LLC
97 N18th Street
Wyandanch, NY 11798

ISBN 13: 978-1-60162-400-0
ISBN 10: 1-60162-400-X

First Trade Paperback Printing January 2014
Printed in the United States of America

10 9 8 7 6 5 4 3 2 1

Distributed by Kensington Publishing Corp.
Submit Wholesale Orders to:
Kensington Publishing Corp.
C/O Penguin Group (USA) Inc.
Attention: Order Processing
405 Murray Hill Parkway
East Rutherford, NJ 07073-2316
Phone: 1-800-526-0275
Fax: 1-800-227-9604

Avenging Alex

by

Lewis Ericson

To my mother who is my heart and soul

It is impossible to suffer without making someone pay for it; every complaint already contains revenge.

—Friedrich Nietzsche

Acknowledgments

Thanks to my screeners and friends who always keep me grounded and on purpose with the vision:

Dianne Hamilton
A.F. Scott
Tracy Carson
Kimberly Perdue-Sims
Tya Baker
Tina Brooks McKinney
Tim Dahl
Alicia McCord
Keithley Huggins
Monica Mitcham-Russell
Aisha Smith
Kirstein Mosley
Tirrell Hestle-Dillard

Thank you to WITSEC (Witness Protection Program).

And finally a big THANK YOU to the editors and staff of Urban Books.

e-mail: ericsonlewis@gmail.com

1

Approximately seven miles west of Pasadena, California, sprawled at the base of the San Gabriel Mountains, was the city of Monrovia. This was the community that was chosen as the location to stash Alexandra Solomon and her mother Jamilah once they were removed from the safe house. Over a year had passed since they'd entered witness protection and Alex was still ill at ease with her new life, and with good reason. There were several agencies involved with her surreptitious transition throughout 2009. For several weeks before leaving Georgia, an excess of documents were signed off on and negotiated in order for the reformed Ms. Solomon to assume a new identity. In the process she was inundated with a barrage of questions regarding her ties to the drug traffic in the southeastern portion of the country. As part of her agreement with the US Attorney's office, she was bound to give sworn depositions and intimate knowledge of the nefarious criminal activities of one Xavier Rivera.

Because the WITSEC program is designed only to take care of a witness's basic living and medical expenses, Alex had to put forth some effort to find other means of supplemental employment. Her company back in Atlanta was dissolved and arrangements had also been made for all of the legitimate business and personal assets she'd amassed as an event planner to be liquidated. Some of the funds went to pay off any debt that remained in her name; the balance moved with her when she entered the program, essentially eliminating all traces of her previous existence. In spite of that, the lingering look of a stranger gave her pause, and every backfiring car gave her a start. Given all that they knew, the federal authorities seemed no closer to apprehending Xavier Rivera than they'd been before she and her mother were relocated. Alex, or Adriane as she was now known, was convinced that if someone as ruthless and resourceful as Rivera wanted to find her, he could. Despite the reassurance of John Chase, the inspector from the US Marshal's office assigned to protect them, Alex tried not to take anything for granted, including her asylum.

The 1,100-square-foot, ranch-styled house that they called home was in a quiet, well-kept subdivision, where people were friendly enough but not overly so, which suited Alex just fine. It was comfortable with its warm colors, contemporary furnishings, plush area rugs, and modern prints that adorned the walls. Neither Alex nor her mother were allowed to keep any photographs that displayed people they had known, or obvious landmarks of places they'd been or lived. Every single one of their personal items and mementos was methodically screened to prevent any violation that would cause them to be ejected from the program.

All the change was more than a bit unsettling for Jamilah Solomon, who hadn't really considered the implications of eradicating her years of history in the United States or those of her homeland in Nigeria. She made a conscious effort to adjust accordingly for the safety of her family.

"Mama, you don't have to do this," Alex stressed.

Despite having been in America for over thirty years you could still hear the thick rich colors of Nigeria when Jamilah spoke. "I not only have to, my daughter, I want to. Besides, what kind of life would I have if I could never see you or my grandchild again?"

Once they settled into their new identities life plodded along at a familiar pace. Adriane (Alex) found a job at an upscale boutique and Janette (Jamilah) tended to her granddaughter, Cerena. Still, the potential threat that loomed over them was never too far away from Alex's mind.

At the sound of a crackling rumble of thunder, Alex threw back the comforter and sprang out of bed. She cautiously pulled the curtain back to see that the wind was blowing a tree branch against the house. A streak of lightning flashed across the sky and illuminated what she thought to be a man watching her from the other side of the street. Was it the same man she'd seen the day before?

A muffled scream clung to the back of her throat as she jerked away from the window and darted to the night-stand next to her bed to retrieve her .380 semiautomatic. It was against the program's policy for her to have a gun in her possession, but she'd decided not to leave her safety completely to chance, or in anyone's hands but her own. Whatever she'd seen was gone when she moved back to the window to get another look. The telephone rang and startled her. She hesitated to answer, but opted to before the noise woke her mother.

"Hello," she whispered tentatively.

"Hey, it's me. I just got your message. Is everything all right?"

Alex peered back toward the window. "Yes . . . uh . . . I mean, no. I think I just saw someone outside."

"You think?"

"I can't be sure, but it looked like someone was watching the house."

"The same man you told me about?"

"I don't know. Maybe."

"Are all the doors and windows locked?"

"Yes."

"Is the alarm set."

"Yes, it's armed."

"I'm on my way. I'll be there in fifteen minutes. Don't open the door to anyone but me. Understand?"

"John, you don't have to—"

"Yes, I do. I'm on my way."

Alex hung up the telephone and held the gun close to her breast. Damsel in distress was not a role she fit comfortably into, but she had to admit she was glad to have a man like John Chase to watch out for her.

Alex threw her head back and tossed her chestnut brown highlighted tresses. The mod pixie hair cut she once sported was longer now, softening the look of her caramel complexion.

Without turning on the light she picked up her terrycloth bathrobe from the foot of the bed, slid into it, and crept slowly across the carpeted floor. She opened the bedroom door and looked up the dark hallway, first one way and then the other, just to satisfy herself that no danger was lurking. She tiptoed from her room to a room directly across the hall. The glow of the nightlight illuminated the pastel clouds and chubby-cheeked angels plastered on the walls surrounding her baby's crib, as if somehow the notion of the inanimate wallpaper was protection enough.

Alex inched closer. She breathed a sigh of relief as she watched her baby sleeping. She leaned in and readjusted the soft white blanket covering her, and caressed the girl's face.

"Alexandra."

Alex jumped nervously and spun around, aiming the gun in her hand at her mother, Jamilah.

The woman shrieked, "Oh, for the love of God."

"Don't sneak up on me like that."

The woman caught her breath. "You know I can't stand those things. Please, put it away."

Alex relaxed and lowered the gun. "I'm sorry. It was raining so hard. I thought I heard something. I just wanted to check on Cerena."

"With a gun?"

"I needed to be sure."

"Did you call John?"

"He called me. He's on his way over."

Jamilah sidled up beside the crib and peered inside. "This precious angel can sleep through just about anything. She reminds me so much of you when you were a baby."

"When I found out I was pregnant with her all I wanted to do was protect her. I thought I could give her a real chance at life."

"You've done that, Omolola. You made the best decision you could have made under the circumstances."

"That's what I thought at the time. Now, I'm not so sure."

"Why? Because of who the father is?"

"I thought I loved him, Mama. He betrayed me in the worst possible way. I should have known he was too weak to handle the world I lived in." Alex sighed. "I should never have trusted him. He's made my life hell. Because of him we've had to give up everything and go into hiding. I remember sitting in that jail cell in Atlanta wondering what I was going to do and how I was going to get out of this. And then this miracle happened."

Alex kissed her daughter's forehead and turned to leave the room. Her mother followed. The girl made a cooing noise and wriggled a bit but didn't wake. Alex put the gun back in its hiding place and proceeded into the kitchen. She pulled a bottle of Grey Goose vodka from the freezer, and filled a glass with ice.

"Would you like a drink?"

The woman waved her hand and shook her head. "What woke you besides the storm, Omolola?"

"Don't you mean Adriane?"

Her mother's expression soured and she grimaced. "I don't care what name those people give you; you will always be my Omolola." Jamilah brushed her hand over her lush, peppery mane and took a seat at the kitchen table.

"I want this nightmare to be over," Alex continued. "I want to stop seeing Xavier Rivera in every shadow." Harkening back to her previous life, she supposed this existence was justifiable recompense for how she and her former associates made others feel when threatened: anxious, scared, and constantly on edge. "Not a day has passed in this last year when I haven't regretted taking Rivera's phone call after Ray died." Alex scoffed. "Just one bad decision after the other."

"Do you think vodka will help you come to terms with the regret and allow you sleep?" Jamilah asked.

"It sure as hell couldn't hurt."

"Omolola, I'm worried about you."

"You don't need to. I'm fine, Mama. Go back to bed."

"Now, how are you going to tell me not to worry? You're not eating. You're not sleeping. I'm going to worry about you as much as you worry about your own child. I just wish I could make this better for you somehow."

"Mama, you've done everything you could possibly do. You gave up your entire life because of me. It's my fault you had to sacrifice so much."

Jamilah stood and went to Alex. She put her arms around her and gave her a big squeeze. "Don't take this all on yourself. It was my decision to come with you. And they're going to find that man, you'll see. We're going to be all right, Alexandra. We have John here to look after us."

"Yes, but for how long? He's got his own life. He's got other cases."

"He's going to be here for as long as we need him. Besides, I have a feeling that man likes you."

"Mama." Alex pulled away, nearly blushing. "What would make you say something like that?"

"I see the way he's been looking at you. It may have been awhile, but I can still tell when a man feels something for a woman."

Alex pondered her mother's words as she savored the alcohol in her glass. "He's just doing a job, and that job does not include having a relationship with the woman he's supposed to be protecting."

"Uh-huh." Jamilah smirked. "I think I will have that nightcap after all." She pulled a glass from the cupboard. "John Chase is a man, and that's all I need to know."

Alex grabbed the bottle and sat down at the table. "Romance is the last thing I need to be thinking about right now, especially with someone like him. I don't have the best track record when it comes to relationships."

Her mother joined her. "Tirrell Ellis is nothing like John Chase, in case you hadn't noticed. Neither was Raymond for that matter."

Alex considered the two men who had the most dramatic impact in her life: Ray Williams, her smooth-talking, now-deceased husband, who thrust the young college girl into a world of drugs, money, and glamour; and then there was the hotheaded Tirrell Ellis who threatened that lifestyle, and who was subsequently responsible for taking it all away.

The doorbell rang and both women gasped and froze in mid-thought. Jamilah clutched the top of her blue satin robe close around her neck and started to get up. Alex reached out her hand to stop her and went ahead of her. She leaned into the peephole, but it was too obscured to make anything out.

"Adriane," the mellow baritone called out. "It's John."

Alex disarmed the alarm and threw open the door as fast as she could unlock it. She'd grown accustomed to the sound of his voice. The presence of the solid, good-looking, dark-skinned, 220-pound, six foot two inch inspector was reassuring. His confidence was one of the things she found most appealing about him. She'd consistently been drawn to that attribute in a man. Her husband was like that; so was Tirrell, at least, in the beginning.

"What have I told you about opening the door without first making sure you know who it is," the man chided.

"You don't think I recognize your voice after all this time?" Alex repressed the urge to smile.

Despite himself, John smiled. He looked over her shoulder and nodded to Jamilah. "Is everybody all right in here?"

"We're fine," Jamilah assured him.

"I checked around the grounds," John continued. "I didn't find anything out of the ordinary."

Alex moved away from the door and allowed him to enter. He stomped his wet shoes on the mat outside before stepping in. Jamilah hurried to the counter and grabbed a handful of paper towels to give to him.

"Thank you." John took the towels and wiped his brow and clean-shaven head.

"Inspector, can I fix you a drink?" Jamilah offered.

"No, I'm fine." He turned his attention to Alex. "Could you make out anything about the man you saw outside?"

"I'm not even sure there was a man," Alex admitted. "It may have been just my imagination playing tricks on me."

"Alexandra," Jamilah injected, "you didn't tell me you saw someone outside."

"Because I'm not even sure I saw anything at all."

"Whatever it was it scared you enough to get John over here."

Alex rubbed her eyes and moved to the kitchen table for her glass. "John, it really wasn't necessary for you to come over here in the middle of the night like this. I'm sorry I dragged you out of bed or whatever."

"You didn't drag me anywhere. I wasn't asleep. You, your mother, and your little girl are my prime concern right now. Until we get Rivera we don't know who's out there who could be after you, so we need to be vigilant. And that includes you all getting used to calling each other by your new names, even when you think you're alone and no one can hear you."

"I know," Alex agreed.

"I just hate being called Janette," Jamilah complained.

"You're gonna have to," John insisted. "If I'm gonna do my job effectively, you have to play your parts in all of this. Otherwise, we may as well lead you right to the slaughter. Xavier Rivera is going to do everything in his power to find you and keep you from testifying. I've gotta do everything I can to keep you safe."

Jamilah interpreted the look that passed between her daughter and the stalwart inspector, and smiled as she poured more vodka into her glass and pretended to yawn. "Well, if you two will excuse me, I believe Miss Janette is finally ready to get back to bed."

"Good night, ma'am."

Alex left the kitchen and returned with a bigger, more suitable bath towel from the linen closet in the hall. "Here. Give me your jacket and you take this."

John peeled off the wet rain slicker, exchanged it for the dry towel, and sat down.

Alex took the raincoat, hung it on a doorknob, and watched him as he rubbed and patted the moisture from his face, arms, and neck. "Are you sure I can't fix you something to drink?"

"I'll take a cup of coffee if it's not too much trouble."

Alex pulled a filter from the cupboard and filled the coffeepot with water. She felt his eyes watching her from behind and shook her head.

"What's wrong?" he asked.

"Nothing. I was just . . . Do you think it's going to be like this forever?"

"What do you mean?"

She turned around, pulling the tie on her robe tighter, and walked over to the table to sit down. She picked up her glass and swirled the remnants of ice with her index finger. "I'm not used to being the one who's afraid all the time. I'm used to having a certain amount of control over my life. I hate that I've allowed myself to be put in a situation for it to be taken away. I can't get over the fact that even when they catch Xavier I still may not be able to go back to the way things were."

John leaned forward, resting his elbows on his thighs with the towel draped around his neck, rubbing hands together. "Look, I know you're scared. It's all right. We've taken every precaution to protect you."

"Do those precautions include you sticking around after he's caught?"

They looked into each other's eyes. The concentration in his gaze caused her to blink and look away. She tossed back the watered-down remains in her glass and went to the counter. "I think the coffee is ready. Cream and two sugars, right?"

John cleared his throat and sat back in the chair. "Right."

Alex poured two cups of coffee and returned to the table. Their eyes darted nervously as they gingerly sipped the hot brew. Neither seemed to want to be caught looking at the other.

"I didn't mean to imply anything by what I said," Alex confessed. "Blame the vodka."

"I think I've heard that song before," John quipped.

Their mutual laughter masked the growing tension.

"I guess this is my lame attempt at getting to know a little more about you after all these months. I mean you've got this huge file with every sordid detail of my life since the day I lost my first tooth."

John put his cup down on the table. "There's not a whole lot you need to know about me."

"Why not? You're not married, are you?"

He averted his gaze.

Alex's eyes widened with surprise; given the fact that he'd been so present all this time she never thought that he might be. "Oh, wow. You are, aren't you? Damn, I must really be slipping. I used to be able to smell a married man from across the room, even if he didn't wear a ring."

She looked at his hand as he absently rubbed the finger where a wedding band had been.

"For the record, I'm separated."

"Separated as in different living arrangements, or separated as in 'we've got our problems but we still sleep together'?"

"It's complicated."

"Isn't it always?" Alex stood up and walked into the adjoining living room. "I can't believe I . . . You know what, it's late. You should probably go home. We'll be okay."

John followed. "I wasn't trying to upset you. I just didn't think my personal life was relevant."

"You're right," Alex snapped. "It's not. I just feel really stupid right now."

"Well, you shouldn't."

"I should have realized from the moment I—"

"From the moment you what?"

"I've depended on you more than I should have, that's all."

"You're supposed to depend on me. Your safety is my job."

"You've made that more than clear."

John sighed, exasperated. "Are you pissed off at me now?"

"More so at myself." Alex walked over to the door where John's damp jacket hung, picked it up, and held it out to him. "As usual, Inspector, you've done an excellent job of looking out for us, but like I said, it's late."

"Alex . . ."

"For the record, the name is Adriane. Remember?"

John lingered for a few seconds longer before leaving the house, and waited in his truck until Alex shut the door.

After locking it, she went around rechecking the windows and doors before returning to the bottle of vodka she'd left on the kitchen table. Curling up at the end of the sofa, she poured another drink, and turned on the television. Her eyelids were heavy with exhaustion. She scanned the channels, fighting the sleep she desperately needed, berating herself for feelings she had no right to have. She waited for the demons that would inevitably invade her dreams.

2

Despite the seemingly relentless rains from the night before it was shaping up to be a pleasantly sunny March morning in Southern California. Alex was awakened by the failed attempts of her mother puttering around in the kitchen trying to be quiet. She pulled herself up off the sofa where she'd finally fallen asleep some time after four in the morning. She looked around the room half dazed and stretched.

"Good mornin', daughter," Jamilah chirped. "I'm sorry I woke you. I didn't know you'd be sleeping out here on the sofa. What happened with you and the inspector last night?"

Alex swept her flat-ironed hair from her face and bristled at the memory of having made a fool of herself. "I don't want to talk about it." She lumbered toward the kitchen table. "How much vodka did I have to drink last night?"

"I found the bottle half empty on the counter this morning. You and John must've had a really good chat."

Alex looked at the hopeful expression in her mother's eyes. "Let's just say John and I came to an understanding."

"What time did he leave?"

"Don't get your hopes up. He didn't stay much longer after you went to bed. Nothing happened. We talked and the honorable inspector finished his coffee and went home."

"How much sleep did you manage to get?"

"Two or three hours I guess."

"Alexandra, why don't you go to your room and go back to bed."

Alex opened the refrigerator and pulled out a carton of orange juice. "I'm fine, Mama."

"You want some coffee? I made a fresh pot."

"No, thanks. I'm just going to take something for this headache and get a hot shower. But first I need to check on Cerena."

"Don't worry about that little darlin'. I've already washed her and changed and fed her."

After downing a couple of aspirin, Alex made her way to her daughter's bedroom. She found her wide awake and happy to see her. "How's my treasure?" Alex cooed. She picked the girl up and walked back toward the kitchen.

"If you're not going to go back to bed I should fix you something to eat," Jamilah said.

"I'm not hungry."

"You have to eat, Omolola. You run out of here five days a week with nothing more than a cereal bar. The least you could do on a beautiful Sunday morning is relax long enough to have a decent breakfast."

"Mama."

"Don't argue with me. You think Cerena wants to grow up with a mother who is nothing more than a bag of bones?"

"All right," Alex acquiesced. "I'll eat."

"Good. Now, leave the baby with me and by the time you're done with your shower I'll have breakfast on the table."

The telephone rang just as Alex was about to hand her daughter over to her grandmother. Jamilah reached for the extension on the wall.

"Hello," she sang. "Oh, good morning, Inspector . . . No, you didn't wake us. We were just getting ready to have breakfast . . . Yes, hold on. She's right here."

Alex vigorously shook her head and waved the phone away. Jamilah ignored her protest. She shoved the receiver into Alex's hand and took the baby.

Alex rolled her eyes and sighed. "Hello."

"Hi. I was just calling to make sure you were all right . . . after last night I mean."

Alex looked over her shoulder to ensure that her mother wasn't listening and drew closer into the corner of the room. "I'm fine. Just a little embarrassed. I shouldn't have asked you anything about your personal life. Like you said it wasn't relevant. I guess the vodka just went to my head. So, you have nothing to worry about."

There was hesitation on the line.

"John?"

"I . . . um . . . I think we need to talk."

"I don't think there's anything for us to talk about. At least not as far as that conversation goes."

"I feel like I really need to get some things out in the open. I'd like a chance to explain."

"I'm not stupid, John. Your 'complication' really isn't that difficult to grasp. Why don't we just leave it at that?"

"I still need to talk to you. Can I come by later?"

"No. I have a lot to do today. I've got errands to run and I'm going to be out for a while."

John sighed. "Can I meet you? We could go to lunch or something?"

"I don't think lunch would be a good idea."

"Then how about someplace like that coffee shop in the Pavilions on West Foothill?"

Alex took a deep breath and exhaled slowly. "Why are you pressing this?"

"Because there are some things that I didn't make clear last night."

Alex didn't respond.

"Are you still there?"

"Fine. I have to go to that pharmacy anyway to pick up Mama's inhalers. I can meet you at noon."

"I'll see you then."

Alex turned to hang up the telephone and spied her mother watching her, smiling. "What?"

"You're meeting John?"

"For coffee. That's all."

"See, I told you he was interested."

"Mama, he's married."

"Married?"

"Technically he says he's separated. Either way there's not a chance in hell we're going to get involved."

"So, why are you meeting him?"

"It's just coffee, all right?"

Alex retreated to her bathroom to shower and change. "It's just coffee" was about as ambiguous as "it's complicated." Despite what she tried to convince herself of, in her heart she was hoping for more.

John was already seated when Alex arrived at the coffee shop. She lingered at the door to pull herself together. Catching her reflection in the glass she brushed the loose hair back behind her ears, smoothed down her camel-colored pencil skirt, and ran her index finger delicately along the bottom line of her freshly applied lipstick. The five foot nine inch fugitive may have assumed a new identity, but her impeccable style was still intact, even on a budget.

When she opened the door the air-conditioned breeze inside the shop countered the warm air outside, causing the material of her burgundy silk blouse to flap against her red-boned complexion, sending a shiver down her spine. She could actually hear her heart pounding. It had been a long time since a man stirred her the way John Chase did. His magnetism was just the right blend of strength and raw sexuality that made him all kinds of irresistible. There was something about the way his expressive brown eyes found hers when he spoke. A man like that could be all consuming, she thought, because he was the type who could tell a lie without missing a beat.

"Hi." He smiled. It was infectious.

"Hi." She gracefully slid her curvaceous frame into the chair facing him and pulled off her designer sunglasses.

"Wow . . . Do you always dress like this just to run errands?"

Alex blushed. "What's wrong with the way that I'm dressed?"

John smiled and shook his head. "Not a complaint. Just an observation. Can I get you something?"

"Iced caramel macchiato."

"Comin' right up."

Alex blew a cleansing breath to allay her anxiety as she watched John's swagger when he went to the counter; blue jeans rarely looked so enticing.

"Here you go. One iced caramel macchiato with extra caramel."

"So, you just took it upon yourself to add extra caramel?"

"You look like an extra caramel kind of girl."

She smirked as her eyes came to rest at the opening of his crisp white button-down shirt revealing a flirtatious hint of the hard smoothness underneath.

"Did you get all your errands taken care of?"

"What?"

"I asked you if you were done with your errands."

"Yes." She took a sip of the iced beverage and steeled herself. "You wanted to talk, so talk."

John ran his index finger and thumb over his neatly trimmed moustache and goatee. "I was running different scenarios in my head, trying to figure out what I wanted to say. Now that you're actually sitting here, I don't quite know where to start."

"You don't seem to be the kind of man who has problems saying what's on your mind, Inspector."

"You'd be surprised."

They sat in silence for a few seconds before John spoke again. "I haven't been completely honest with you. Despite what I said before, you're not just another job to me. I tried not thinking about it. I even considered turning you over to another agent—"

"Turning me over? You make it sound like I was some sort of experiment or class project."

"That's not what I meant."

"Then what exactly do you mean?"

John sighed heavily before continuing. "I pride myself on the ability to keep my personal life and my work separate. In this line of work it's dangerous to blur the lines. I should be able to handle my feelings a lot better than I've been able to do lately. Look, I don't know when it happened or how, but somewhere over these past few months you got to me."

"I got to you?"

"You know what I'm talking about."

"John, you've read my file. You know I'm not your garden-variety girl next door."

"I know what you are, and I know who you are."

"And that's not enough to keep this line of yours from being blurred?"

"I'm here, aren't I?"

Alex lowered her gaze. She wanted to light up, but opted to remain aloof. Other than the protective aspect of what there was between them there remained the issue of a wife. "Tell me about your separation. That is part of the reason you asked me to meet you here, isn't it?"

"You're not making this easy for me."

"If you wanted it easy you wouldn't have asked me to come."

John rubbed his hand over his face and sat back in his chair. "I've been married almost ten years. I had a good marriage, or so I thought. But when you take each other for granted for so long you wake up one day and you come to the realization that you've grown apart. Somewhere the relationship derailed and you don't have a clue how to get back on track, or if you even want to."

"How long have you been separated?"

"John," a shrill voice called from the direction of the counter.

They both turned and saw a sallow, blonde woman headed toward their table. Alex noticed John's agitation and rested her elbows on the table and leaned in.

"I thought that was you," the woman noted, taking Alex in with a glance.

John gallantly or nervously stood up, Alex wasn't sure which.

"Caren, how's it going?"

"It's going well. I'm here spending the day with my mother-in-law." The woman looked at John as if she'd caught him with his hands in the proverbial cookie jar. "How're Lorraine and the kids? I haven't seen them since we moved."

"They're fine."

The woman eyed Alex again.

John fumbled through an introduction. "Caren Wallace, this is Adriane Sullivan."

"Nice to meet you, Ms. Sullivan." The woman nodded as if she knew more than she did.

Annoyed by the implication in her tone, Alex flashed a patronizing smile and nodded back.

Hearing her order being called drew the woman's attention back to the counter. "Well, that's me. I guess I'd better go. Tell Lorraine I'll give her a call. Bill and I need to have you guys over for dinner soon. I can't wait to show you what we've done with the new place."

John vacillated between a smile and a grimace. He waited until the woman was out of the coffee shop before sitting back down. He glanced at Alex and rubbed his hands over his bald pate and down the sides of his face.

"Lorraine? I take it that's your wife?"

"Yeah," John responded sheepishly.

"And this Caren woman is probably on the phone to her right now."

"Probably."

"So, you were starting to tell me about this train wreck of a marriage and the separation that apparently no one else knows about."

"Because it's nobody's business. Look, the separation was what my wife wanted."

"You didn't?"

"Not at first. I thought maybe we had something worth fighting for."

"And now you don't?"

"We started having problems a long time before we separated."

"You were assigned to my case last December. Were you still with her then?"

"I stayed through Christmas for the kids. I moved out of the house after the New Year."

"Ah, yes, the complication. How many children do you have?"

"Two. My oldest is eight, and I have a five-year-old girl."

Alex picked up her purse and scooted back from the table. John reached out and took her hand. She jerked away. "Don't."

"Can you please sit down?"

"Why?"

"Because this is not the way I wanted to tell you."

"You love your wife. You're having problems. Every marriage has problems; that doesn't mean it's over with the two of you. So, what else is there to say?" Alex started to the door and John followed her and grabbed her arm.

"Can we please finish our conversation like two adults?"

"Let's not and say we did." Alex pulled her arm from John's grasp. She looked at the pleading in his eyes and sighed heavily. "All right, fine."

They stepped outside the coffee shop and stood under a tree on the sidewalk.

"I moved out of the house. My . . . Lorraine and the kids are still there. I'm staying at my brother's place."

"If that's true, why does that woman think you and your wife are still together?"

"I don't give a damn what Caren Wallace or anybody else thinks."

"It didn't seem that way when you saw her."

"Because she caught me off-guard. I was concentrating on you. I wasn't thinking about running into anybody I know."

Alex scoffed. "Maybe we'd both be better off if you'd just stick to doing what you do best. Can we go back to the way things were and pretend we never had this conversation?"

"Now that the door is open I'm just trying to be upfront with you."

"Really?"

"Out of respect, I've been trying to keep my distance and keep my head on straight so the way I was starting to feel about you wouldn't get in the way of making sure you were safe. That was my number one priority. It still is."

"Then what do you want from me, John?"

"I know this is crazy. But, can you at least admit that there is something more going on here? Isn't that why you were talking the way you were last night?"

"I'd been drinking."

"C'mon, don't do that. You and I both know it was more than that."

"So, you want me to stroke your ego and tell you that all I can think about is you too."

"That's not what this is about."

"Then what is it?"

"Just tell me that I'm full of shit and you don't feel anything at all and I'll back off."

"Hand me off to another agent?"

"Yeah, if that's what it takes. If that's what you want."

Before Alex could formulate or articulate a rejection John's cell phone rang and broke them apart.

"Answer it," Alex snapped. "It's probably your wife."

John glanced at the caller ID and hesitated a few moments longer. "What is it, Lorraine? Slow down. I can't understand you. What happened?"

Alex shook her head, turned, and walked away. John moved to block her, but she shoved him back and continued to the parking lot. She jumped in her car and started the ignition. John darted out in front of her as she threw it in drive, causing her to break hard. She thrust forward and the packages on the front seat flew to the floor.

"Move," she yelled, rolling down the window.

"Not until we finish this."

"I've heard all I need to. Now, get the hell out of my way!"

She blasted the car horn and he threw up his hands and stepped aside. The tires on her Honda Civic screamed out of the parking lot and onto the street.

"Of all the fuckin' nerve," Alex spat as she came to a stop. "What the hell does he take me for? I'm not about to be some slam piece for his macho ass! I can't believe I was actually starting to . . ."

A car horn blared from behind her when the traffic light changed and she floored the accelerator and peeled through the intersection. She was angrier for the vulnerability that she hated in herself than John's seemingly ill-timed open-heart confession. Her pulse quickened and both hands gripped the steering wheel. "What the hell is wrong with me?"

3

John bolted into the emergency room and quickly found his wife, Lorraine, with their eight-year-old son, John Michael. The boy had his arm in a cast.

"What happened?"

"He's fine," the woman said coolly. "He fell out of a tree and broke his arm, that's all."

"What is the doctor saying? Where is he? I want to talk to him."

"John, he's fine. The doctor said everything should be back to normal in about six weeks."

"You made it sound a lot worse over the phone."

The woman ran her slender fingers through her stylishly shagged ginger-colored bob, and sucked in her cheeks. "I thought it was, that's why I called you. It's nice to know you can still put your family first on occasion."

John chose to ignore the dig and stooped down to attend to his son. "How're you feeling, buddy?"

With the exception of the boy's bluish gray eye color set against his mulatto hue, his African American heritage dominated his features.

"It hurts a little," the boy responded. "I was playin' in the tree house with Christopher and he pushed me."

"He pushed you?" John glared back up at his wife. "You weren't watching them?"

"They were playing in the back yard like they always do. I was in the house with Chloe. I can't be in two places at the same time."

"Where's Chloe?"

"I left her with Mrs. Emerson. Is that all right with you?"

"Mom, can we go home now?" the boy whined.

"Yes, sweetie. We're going."

"Are you coming too, Dad?"

John looked into his wife's sparkling blue eyes. "I'll be right behind you, son."

After seeing his wife and son to her car, John ran and jumped into his truck. He tapped on the Bluetooth device hanging from his ear as he drove off and tried to call Alex. She didn't answer. He didn't leave a message.

John pulled up in the drive of the custom-bricked, split-level house in Pasadena he used to share with his wife. He sat in his Ram pickup truck for a few minutes contemplating the scene they were certain to have once he went inside. Time and lack of communication began to erode what he'd once considered to be a solid foundation between him and the former Rose Bowl Queen long before Alex Solomon entered the picture.

When he threw open the door of his truck a little girl with sandy-colored curls and a face dotted with freckles bolted from the house. "Daddy!"

He swept her up in his arms. The soft whiskers of his goatee tickled her neck as he kissed her.

"Daddy, are you coming to see me dance on Thursday?"

John feigned surprise. "You're dancing?"

"Yes." She nodded.

"Are you the best dancer?"

"Yes."

"Well, in that case I have to be there, don't I?"

"Yes." The little girl hugged his neck and he continued inside. His wife met them at the door.

"Where's John Michael?"

"He's up in his room."

John put the little girl down and started for the stairs.

"Where are you going?" the woman asked.

"I'm gonna go up and see my son if that's all right with you," John answered evenly. He didn't wait for a response and bounded up the staircase. He found his son amid a cache of the latest electronic gadgets that any boy his age would envy. He looked up helplessly. John pitied the boy's attempt to manipulate the controls of his Xbox. "It's going to be pretty hard to beat me now that your arm is all busted up like that."

"I'll betcha I still can though."

"Well, maybe we should see what you got after you get some rest." John took the controller from the boy's hand and laid it to the side. He examined his cast. "Does it hurt really bad?"

"A little," the boy responded.

"Why don't you try to take a little nap and maybe it'll feel better when you wake up."

Without argument the boy awkwardly climbed up on the bed and lay on his back, looking up at John. "Dad, can I ask you something?"

"Yeah, sure."

"Mom says that you might be moving back home, is that true?"

"Tell you what, why don't we talk about that later, okay?" John ran his hand over the boy's bushy mane and kissed his forehead. "No matter what happens I love you, you know that, right?"

"I love you too, Dad."

John left his son's room and made his way back downstairs to find his wife perched at the bar that divided the large living room area from a formal dining room.

"Where's Chloe?"

"She's in the family room."

"I'd better go say good-bye."

"Good-bye? Rushing back to your girlfriend so soon?"

John stopped in his tracks and turned to face his wife.

"I hear she's pretty."

John scoffed. "I didn't figure Caren Wallace would waste much time. Does she have you on speed dial?"

"I thought we were going to try to make this marriage work."

"We did try, remember? It didn't work."

"And you're wasting no time moving on."

"The separation was your idea. Now you're telling the kids that I'm moving back in?"

"It's what they want, John. It's what I want."

"You sure about that?"

"I see you're not wearing your ring. Are you sure a separation isn't what you've wanted all along?"

"Lorraine, let's not do this right now, okay?"

"Do what, John?"

"Have another fight. Say some shit we won't be able to take back."

"You never answered the question, John."

"What question?"

"About the woman you're rushing off to be with."

"I'm not rushing off to be with anybody, Lorraine. I'm working a case and you know I can't talk about it."

"Oh, right. She's one of your cases? Well, that explains everything, doesn't it?"

"I've gotta go."

"I thought you wanted to say good-bye to Chloe."

John huffed and rubbed his hand over his mouth before exiting to the family room. He emerged a minute later and continued to the door without another word to Lorraine.

"John, wait." Lorraine hopped off the stool and went after him. "Please stay. The kids need you. I need you." She pressed into him.

He swallowed his emotions and backed away. "You know I'm not going to stop being a father to my kids."

"You haven't been here five minutes and you can't wait to get away."

"I'll come back when I have more time."

"Time." The woman sighed. "That's always been your problem, hasn't it, John? Not enough time for you to play superhero and be a father and husband, too. Do you at least have time to show up to your daughter's recital this week, or will one of your cases take precedence again?"

"I promised Chloe I would be there."

Lorraine flashed a hopeful smile as she leaned in and brushed her lips softly against his. "I don't want this. I want you to come home where you belong. I want my husband back."

"I'll call later to check on John Michael." John quickly exited and sat in his truck for several seconds before pulling off. There was a time not so long ago that he would have welcomed the embrace of his wife without question, but too much time had passed while he waited, and there was someone else pulling at his heart now.

Alex stared at the caller ID, questioning whether to answer. When she decided it was too late; the call went to voicemail, but still there was no message.

"Was that John again?"

"Yeah."

"How long are you going to ignore his calls?"

Alex sighed and threw her head back. "I made a fool out of myself today, Mama."

"Why? Because you have feelings for a married man?"

"No. Well, yeah, that's part of it. And, the fact that I had the nerve to get mad when she called him, as if I had any rights to the man."

Jamilah came from the kitchen with two glasses of iced tea, gave one to Alex, and sat next to her on the sofa. "He laid this on you, Alexandra. You didn't go to him."

"Is that supposed to make me feel better?"

"Well, you said that he as much as told you that his marriage is over. He's not even living with the woman. Whatever she did to lose him isn't your problem."

"Getting divorced and already being divorced are two completely different things, Mama. Besides, I don't want to be any man's rebound. And I have no intention of being the other woman in his drama."

"It's not as if you're coming between them. You said he told you that they were over long before you came along."

"Yes, but it was his wife's idea to end things."

"So?"

"So, what happens when she changes her mind?"

"What happens if she doesn't?"

They turned their attention to the baby monitor as Cerena's cries rang out. "Uh-oh, somebody's up from their nap." Jamilah set her glass down on the coffee table and pushed up from the sofa.

Alex stood up as well. "Mama, I'll get her. You've had her all afternoon."

"I don't mind. You sit there and think about what you're going to do when John calls back. Or maybe you shouldn't wait."

Alex sat back down and sipped her tea. She picked up her cell phone and flipped it open, contemplating calling him. When she started to dial she caught sight of a figure through the open drapes at the window, moving about in the yard in front of the house. She put her glass down and hurried over. Pulling back the sheer, she spied an older-model white-paneled van parked at the curb. She glanced around the yard, but she didn't see anyone. A knock at the door made her jump.

"Hello," called a male voice from the other side of the door.

Alex stood frozen between the large bay window and the unsecured door. The knocking continued. When Jamilah came up the hallway from the back of the house holding the baby Alex felt compelled to move. She held her index finger to her mouth, signaling her mother to be still, and she crept to the door.

"Who is it?" she asked sternly, securing the dead bolt.

"I'm looking for the Johnsons," the man answered.

"You have the wrong house," Alex barked.

"I know I've got the right address. Are you sure there's no Paul Johnson who lives here?"

Alex eyes darted toward Jamilah, who was rocking the baby to keep her from fussing. "Yes, I'm sure."

"Do you know where he lives?"

"I don't know any Paul Johnson. Now get away from my door before I call the police."

"Look, lady, there's no need to be hostile. I'm just looking for a friend of mine."

"I have a gun and if you don't leave I'm going to use it." Alex's throat went dry as she stood and listened. There was no response. Seconds dragged by before she heard the roar of the van's engine. She hurried back to the window. The van pulled away before she could see who it was.

"Call John," Jamilah insisted.

"I can't."

"This is no time for your stubborn pride, Omolola. You have to call John."

After pulling herself together Alex stepped to her mother and took the baby. "Mama, I'm sure it was nothing. It was just some guy who obviously had the wrong address. I can't call John every time somebody knocks at the door."

"You don't know if that was just somebody. You need to call John. That's what he's here for."

Jamilah was right. The man at the door seemed pretty insistent that someone lived there who didn't. She had to report anything suspicious, no matter how benign. She picked up her cell phone and dialed.

"John, it's me."

It had been like every other time before. When Alex made a distress call, John Chase came running. Alex was clear on the fact that this was his job. Maybe in the midst of this convoluted milieu of impending discovery and danger lay the only reasons either of them was attracted to the other. In a matter of minutes John was joined by his partner, Harley Donovan, and the local police. The doorknob was dusted for fingerprints, and the yard was checked for any evidence the trespasser may have inadvertently left behind.

"I didn't see him," Alex admitted. "I was sitting over there on the sofa and I saw this shadow move across the yard. The next thing I knew he was knocking and then when I threatened him with my . . ." She stopped short of confessing that she had a gun. "When I told him I was going to call the police he ran off."

The sinewy Harley Donovan curiously scratched the neatly trimmed stubble on his face. "You didn't see the license plate of the van?"

"No. The van was old and white. It was banged up and rusted in spots. But I didn't get a look at the plate numbers."

"We got some smudged prints from the door," a female officer reported as she entered the house. "We also lifted a decent shoeprint outside the kitchen window at the side of the house."

"Would you all please watch where you're stepping?" Jamilah cautioned them. "You're tracking all over my rugs and I just cleaned."

The officer apologized. John turned his attention back to Alex. "Did he say anything?"

"He said he was looking for somebody named Paul Johnson."

"Was there anything distinctive about his voice? Did he have an accent or anything like that?"

"Not that I could tell."

"He didn't get into the house?"

"He didn't get the chance. I was out earlier and when I came back in I forgot to lock the dead bolt."

Donovan, who'd been glancing around the room at nothing in particular, chimed in. The resonance in his voice and cadence of his words informed of his breeding from the Lone Star State. "You were out? Where did you go?"

Alex cut John a side glance and then addressed the man. "I went to the pharmacy on West Foothills to pick up my mother's albuterol."

Jamilah, who'd pulled out a broom and dustpan and made her way back in from the kitchen, nodded her confirmation.

"Were you alone?" Donovan pressed. "You didn't notice this van while you were out, or following you from the pharmacy when you left?"

"No," Alex snapped.

"Sorry," Donovan apologized. "Just tryin' to get the details."

Alex combed her fingers through her tousled tresses and wrapped her arms around herself. "I . . . I'm sorry. I know you're just trying to do your job. I had a lot of things on my mind when I left and I wasn't really paying attention."

John interrupted. "Donovan, why don't you get those prints expedited through the system. The sooner we know something the easier everyone can breathe. I'll hang back here."

"You sure?"

"Yeah. There's a patrol car out looking for any signs of the van. There's not a whole lot else we can do at the moment."

"Okay. I'll go down to the office and see if anything turns up. I'll keep you posted."

Jamilah leaned out the door as John's partner and the police departed. She noted the people who were out jogging or walking dogs gathering to look and speculate.

A particularly curious neighbor craned her neck from her front step and yelled across the street, "Is there anything wrong, Janette?"

"Nothing for you to worry about, Ernie Mae," Jamilah responded with a generic smile and wave. "Everything's fine." She closed the door and grimaced. "Inspector, do you think there's anything to this man coming to the house?"

"Can't say just yet," John replied. "We'll see what comes of the fingerprints. This could all be random, somebody with the wrong address."

"What if I did see a man outside the other night? What if this was the man?" Alex's voice rose barely above a whisper.

"Alex." John caught himself and glanced over his shoulder. "Adriane, I don't want to scare you any more than you already are, but if it was one of Xavier's men I don't think he would've stopped with a knock on the door. And I don't think anyone who works for him would've been so careless as to leave fingerprints behind that could be identified."

"I thought you said none of Xavier Rivera's people knew where we are," Jamilah interjected.

"I am positive that you're safe," John replied.

Alex looked into John's eyes. "For all our sakes I hope you're right."

Jamilah excused herself to go check on the baby. Alex slowly sank onto the sofa. John sat beside her. "I was a cop for the LAPD for four years. I've been doing this job for six, and I haven't lost anyone I was assigned to protect. I don't intend for you to be the first."

Alex raised her head and smiled. "That's comforting." She swallowed back a cluster of emotions surging through her as she looked into his soulful eyes. "Have you always wanted to do this kind of work?"

"Not always. When I was growin' up I didn't really think I had any real future outside Compton. I saw a lot of friends either get locked up, or killed, and I was going down that same path until this cop who used to hang in my neighborhood knocked some sense into me."

Alex was pleasantly distracted by John's conversational tone. "You were a troublemaker?"

"I got popped for breaking into these houses when I was thirteen."

"You're kidding, right?"

"It was pretty stupid, but that's what the kids I hung out with did back then," John mused.

Alex laughed. "So you were a little hustler, huh?"

"Headed straight to juvie."

"And this cop steered you in the right direction?"

"Yeah. Hank Mitchell was the first man I'd met who had such an impact on my life. He kept me out of the gangs."

John became animated as he continued. "Hank was like this big, muscular dude who used to be a Marine and he didn't take crap from anybody. He used to tell me that he was gonna bust my ass if I didn't get my shit together, but he was cool as hell. He started shooting ball with me and my older brother on Saturdays when he wasn't on duty."

"What happened to him?"

John smiled. "He ended up marrying my mom when I was fourteen. Hank is the reason I wanted to be a cop. He tried to talk me into pursuing a law degree instead. I got into a community college for a couple of years and then managed to get into USC. After I graduated I met . . ."

"You met Lorraine?"

"Yeah, and I ended up being a cop anyway. I could tell Hank was proud of me regardless. I don't know why I'm telling you all this, but you wanted to know some stuff about me, so there it is."

"Well, I'm glad he was there for you. Otherwise, you couldn't be here for me."

"That's true." John gently touched her chin, turned her to face him, and leaned into her. Their kiss was tentative. His lips were full, soft, warm. "I'm sorry," John said. "I don't know why I did that."

Alex pulled away. She moved to the window and stared blankly at the unmarked patrol car driving conspicuously up the street, and her neighbors going on with their days as if the happenings at her address barely registered concern.

"I can't do this, John. We can't . . ."

"Yeah . . . I know." John stood and stepped up behind her.

Alex closed her eyes, feeling the heat of his hands on her shoulders. She entertained his touch for as long as she could before pulling away. "You have to go."

"Yeah," John agreed. "I should go check and see if Donovan came up with anything. I'll call you later."

She watched him walk to his truck, resisting the urge to run out and call him back, cursing herself for her weakness. Before driving off he looked back up at her and smiled. There was a certain comfort in his eyes. She wanted to believe he would protect her at all cost, perhaps beyond reason. But would it be the marshal who came to her aid, or the man?

4

Jamilah scoured the produce section of the farmers' market, sniffing, plucking, and squeezing peaches, melons, and oranges, taking care to select the ripest and freshest of the lot. She shook her head, watching her greedy shopping companion trailing behind her, picking at a stem of unwashed seedless grapes, and popping them in her mouth.

"What?" The woman scoffed; her voice was husky from excessive smoking.

Jamilah chuckled. "You do know you have to pay for those, right?"

"Girl, please. They're here to be sampled. How am I supposed to know if they're sweet enough to buy if I don't try a few?"

"A few? You've eaten almost a whole bag's worth."

"Humph!" Ernie Mae Hudson was a stout, fair-skinned woman with short hair that was more orange than the reddish tint she was going for. She was one of the few women Jamilah had befriended since being displaced. "Girl, don't look now, but I think that man over there is watching us."

Jamilah turned. "Who?"

Ernie Mae slapped Jamilah's arm. "I said don't look."

"Please, I couldn't care less about some man. But, you're welcome to him if you want him."

Ernie Mae tossed the bare stem to the ground and brushed her hands together and adjusted her substantial bosom. "I think I'm more his type anyway. You're a little too old maid."

Jamilah pulled her glasses from her face, letting them dangle from the chain around her neck. She caught her reflection in a mirror over the vegetable bin, pursed her lips, and smoothed down her loose hair.

"I told you to do somethin' with yourself," Ernie Mae chided. "You could have put on lipstick or somethin'. Just 'cause we were goin' to the market don't mean we can't look nice. You don't know who might be lookin' at you."

"I didn't come out here to meet anybody," Jamilah protested. She didn't want to admit that her friend was right. Her bronzed complexion was wholesome enough, but she was in agreement that a little makeup wouldn't have hurt. She could have fixed up a bit even if it was just to go to the farmers' market. Since the death of her husband some thirteen years prior, she hadn't really taken much of an interest in another man. It wasn't as if she let herself go, she just didn't go out of her way to attract them. Still, as her daughter reminded her, she was as beautiful as ever despite a few more gray hairs and wrinkles that honored her age.

"Oooh, he's comin' over here," Ernie Mae said excitedly.

"Excuse me," the man said, nodding his head in a gentlemanly manner. "You look very familiar to me."

Ernie Mae rolled her eyes, insulted that the man looked right past her to Jamilah. "You couldn't have come up with anything better than that," she scoffed.

"My name is Ade Obafemi."

Jamilah suppressed a smile and brushed her hand over her hair. "Janette Sullivan."

"Very nice to meet you, Janette Sullivan."

The robust man's coarse white hair complemented his dark features. There appeared to be wisdom and kindness in his expression, along with a mischievous twinkle that told of a well-spent youth.

"Obafemi," Jamilah repeated.

"I am from Nigeria."

Jamilah smiled. "Well, so am I."

"I've been in the United States for a few years now from Kandula," the man continued.

"I wasn't too far from there." Jamilah smiled. "I lived in Abuja."

"My son lives there," the man noted.

"You're married?"

"Widower."

"Oh, I'm sorry. I'm a widow myself."

"Excuse me," Ernie Mae snapped. "I hate to break up the dead spouse club, but there is another person standing here."

"This is my friend Ernie Mae Hudson."

The man nodded. "My apologies."

The woman elbowed Jamilah's side. "We need to get goin', don't we, Janette?"

The man took Jamilah's hand. "It was a pleasure meeting you, Janette Sullivan. Perhaps we could meet for tea some afternoon. I don't live far from here."

Ernie Mae shrieked. "You don't expect her to come to your house, do you?"

"No, not at all. I didn't mean to imply—"

"Don't mind her, Mr. Obafemi," Jamilah injected.

His expression flushed with embarrassment. "Perhaps I could call on you soon."

"There's a small park not far from here that I go to. Sometimes twice a week," Jamilah offered. "I don't suppose there would be any harm should I see you there at some point."

"I would like that very much."

Unlike Alex, Jamilah wasn't as guarded as she perhaps should have been. She saw no harm in an innocent meeting. No threat of peril prowling in darkness or behind corners. No cause for misgiving. Seeing how the man's attention affected Ernie Mae Hudson was a silent victory to be sure, one that she would delight in sharing with Alex later.

Given her own anxieties Alex was less than amused at her mother's tale over dinner.

"You should have seen Ernie Mae's face." Jamilah laughed. "Green is not that woman's color."

"I can't believe you flirted with a stranger like that."

"I did no such thing, Alexandra. I was just being cordial."

"Mama, you didn't know anything about him."

"I said hello to the man; I didn't invite him to bed."

Silence fell between the two as they sat across from one another at the table. Alex picked at the meatloaf on her plate, realizing that there may have been no real cause for suspicion of some innocuous older man. "I'm sorry, Mama."

Jamilah reached across the table and patted Alex's hand. "It's all right. I know we can't be too careful, but we can't close ourselves off completely either."

"I know," Alex conceded. "I need to stop looking for trouble. So, tell me more about this man you met."

Jamilah smiled. "His name is Ade and he's from Kandula. When I told him I was from Nigeria as well he—"

"Wait. What! You told him where you were from?"

"Omolola, don't be so alarmed. He seemed to be a perfectly respectable gentleman. I doubt very much that he's some trained assassin."

Alex sighed. "Oh, Mama, I just get so freaked out. I'm sorry. I need to calm down."

"Why don't you call John?"

"Why?"

"So you can talk to him. See where things really stand between him and his wife."

Alex scoffed. "No. I'm not going to do that. I don't beg and I don't grovel."

"Then why don't you go out and find some nice young man to occupy your time. You're a beautiful woman. If John Chase is not the man for you then there's someone out there who is."

"You're looking at a long list of state and federal charges that could have you doing time until you're eligible to collect Social Security, assuming that the program is still around when you get out. If that scares you, it should. I don't see a man like Xavier Rivera sitting on the clock waiting to see how all of this plays out. Give us something we can nail him on, Ms. Solomon, and we could put you in protective custody until we get Rivera out of the picture. Give me something to work with, Ms. Solomon."

A gunshot rang out and Alex's eyes sprung open. She bolted straight up in the bed, swallowing back a scream. "It was just a dream," she heaved. "That's all it was." She glanced toward the illuminated clock on the nightstand. "Five o'clock." She groaned and rolled over, rearranging the pillows, hoping to snag a few more hours of sleep; it was not forthcoming.

She rolled out of bed, yawned, stretched, and went to check on her daughter. Relieved at the calm of the house, she readjusted the baby's blanket and made her way to the kitchen to make coffee. There was a quiet in the early morning that made her feel at ease. John informed her that nothing suspicious had come back from the man's fingerprints that were run through the system. He also told her the house the man was actually looking for was one street over and Paul Johnson had only just moved in. That allayed her fear all the more, knowing that her whereabouts had not been discovered. She sat oddly content at the table, sipping her coffee, listening to the birds chirping from a tree branch outside the window, and flipping through the *Monrovia Weekly*.

"Good morning," Jamilah sang as she came around the corner into the kitchen. "You're up early. I heard you stirrin' around last night. What time did you get to bed?"

"John called a little after eleven. I really didn't want to sleep until I heard from him."

"What did he say?"

"They tracked down the guy who came to the house. The only thing that turned up was some unpaid parking tickets, and some sort of record of a domestic dispute with his girlfriend. Turns out the man he was looking for had just moved into a house one block over."

"Well, that's good, but what did he say about the two of you?"

"Mama, stop. Nothing is going to happen between us."

"I'm not crazy, Omolola. Something is already happening whether you want to own up to it or not."

"Well, he's married and he has a family and that's the end of that."

"I hear your head talkin', but I don't think your heart agrees."

Before Alex could put forth any sort of rebuttal Cerena's cry interrupted, and she got up and went to look after her.

"Shhhh . . . it's all right, baby girl. Mommy's here. Oooh, you're getting so big." She picked the girl up from the crib, cleaned her up, and changed her soiled diaper. The girl was instantly calmed by her mother's touch. "You're hungry aren't you? Yes, you are."

Alex went to the kitchen to find that Jamilah had already prepared the bottle. She took the bottle and went back to sit in the living room. Cradled in her mother's arms Cerena hungrily drank the formula while gazing up at her with her big hazel eyes. Alex caressed Cerena's silken curls and was struck by her intent stare, dismissing the notion that Tirrell was looking back at her. She felt tears welling up in her eyes and blinked them away. Since discovering she was pregnant, and especially after Cerena's birth, she'd experienced so many foreign and unexpected emotions that had taken some getting used to because she never considered herself particularly maternal. The edge she had survived on for so many years had been dissolved by a tidal wave of angst and hormones. Her own preservation was no longer paramount, which added to her anxiety. The need to control her environment had taken on a new dimension. The welfare of her child needed to be put above all else. Jamilah was an example of the sacrifice motherhood required of her, having given up her friends and the familiarity of her home in New York to follow her daughter into exile.

"Okay, let me have my granddaughter. I've made you some breakfast."

"Mama, I'm not hungry."

"Don't be foolish, Omolola. You can see to your baby, but I can't see about mine? Come on now. Give me Cerena and you go in there and eat."

Alex passed the baby to her mother, went to the kitchen, and sat down to a plate of bacon and blueberry pancakes. She was hungrier than she realized. Before she knew it her plate was empty. The sound of Jamilah's singing from the living room brought a smile to her face as she cleared the table. Alex peered inside to see Jamilah rocking Cerena and making the funny faces she used to make when she'd sung the same song to her so many years before.

"'L'abe igi orombo . . . N'ibe l'agbe nsere wa . . . Inu wa dun, ara wa ya . . . L'abe igi orombo . . . Orombo, orombo . . . Orombo, orombo.' Do you remember, Omolola?"

"'Under the Orange Tree,'" Alex recalled. "How could I forget? You sang it to me practically every night before I would fall asleep."

"Cerena loves it too."

Alex walked over and hugged them. "She loves her *nnenne,* and so do I. I don't know what I would have done if I didn't have you here."

"Look, I want to show you something." Jamilah put Cerena on the floor and stepped back a few feet from her. "Come here, beautiful girl. Come to *Nnenne.*"

Cerena pushed up on her knees, bouncing and bobbing back and forth. Her saliva-lined lips babbled disconnected vowels and consonants as her grandmother clapped and encouraged her.

"That's right. Come to *Nnenne.*"

Alex was astounded when Cerena began to crawl toward them. "Oh, my God, when did this happen?"

"She's been trying for days."

Alex reached down and lifted the girl to her feet. Cerena gripped her index fingers with her tiny hands and launched into a few timid steps. Tears brimmed in Alex's eyes. She swept Cerena up in her arms and kissed her.

Jamilah swayed side to side. "Sing with me, Omolola."

"No. I can't sing."

"Come now, of course you can."

"I don't have your voice."

"You have *a* voice; that's all that matters to this one."

Alex reluctantly twirled around singing (off key), as Jamilah clapped, laughed, and joined in, correcting her on the words she mispronounced.

That moment was as close to normal as most anything else she could have done.

5

La Bella was the chic women's boutique in Pasadena, where those who craved the excess but not necessarily the clamor of Rodeo Drive came to shop. Even though she would have preferred the role of shopper over that of sales associate, Alex's keen fashion sense made her a natural for such an establishment. It wasn't the event planning business that allowed her the cover of a high-profile mover and shaker out of Atlanta, but it offered her enough of a discount to afford to look the part.

"Hi, it's Margot calling from La Bella. The dresses you ordered last week came in. Great, we'll see you soon." The statuesque, overly tanned brunette with a mod-styled Mohawk hung up the telephone and busied herself behind the counter.

Alex had just finished dressing the display windows with some of the newly arrived merchandise. "What do you think?" She held a brightly colored Italian silk scarf against her blouse and turned toward the woman at the counter.

"I like. It looks good on you."

"I'm actually thinking about buying it for my mother. Her birthday's next week."

"Adriane, she's going to love it."

Alex smirked and glanced at the price tag of the scarf. "Three hundred dollars. On second thought, maybe I better wait until it goes on sale."

The woman laughed. "Hey, do you think you can handle things around here for a while? Celeste called and she's still in that meeting in L.A. She asked me to take these receipts to the bank before noon."

"Sure. No problem. Go ahead."

The woman grabbed her purse and a stack of bank receipts and started toward the door. "I'm gonna stop at Jamba Juice on the way back. Do you want me to pick you up anything?"

"No, I'm good."

"Oh, and there's a customer coming in to pick up some dresses she ordered last week. They're marked in a bag in the back."

"No problem. I'll take care of it."

The woman breezed out of the store and Alex made her way over to assist a customer rifling through a rack of skirts. "May I help you with anything?"

"I love this color. Do you have it in a sixteen?"

Alex pressed her lips together and sized up the woman, who was obviously much larger than she admitted to. Still, she didn't want to take her question for granted and decided to be tactful. "Is it going to be for you or a gift for someone else?"

"No, I'm buying it for me."

Alex assisted the woman with her futile search, knowing full well that, other than accessories, La Bella didn't cater to fuller-figured clientele.

"Ma'am, may I recommend a few other stores that I'm certain will have what you're looking for? I'd be happy to call ahead for you."

The woman gave Alex the once-over. "Are you insulting me?"

"No, ma'am. I just thought—"

"You thought what?"

A bell clattered on the door and another patron entered, allowing Alex an escape. "Excuse me for minute." She turned and rolled her eyes. "Hi, welcome to La Bella."

"I got a call from Margot. She told me that some dresses I ordered had come in."

"Margot stepped out for a while, but I'd be happy to help. Can I get your name?"

"Lorraine Chase."

"Chase?"

"That's right. Lorraine Chase."

"I'll um . . . I'll go get your things from the back." Alex's heart raced as she made her way to the back of the store. *This can't be John's wife,* she thought. *There's got to be more than one Lorraine Chase in Pasadena.*

She peered through the curtain separating the stock room from the rest of the store and watched curiously as the pristine redhead moved about, holding various items up to herself in front of a full-length mirror. Finding the dresses that had been set aside, Alex couldn't resist opening the bag to check out the woman's purchases.

"Size four. Bitch."

Alex quickly zipped the bag back up and carried it out to the counter. The trendy female joined her, plopping down various accessories she wanted to add to her purchase; among them was the Italian scarf Alex had admired earlier. "Can I help you find anything else?"

The woman opened her wallet to retrieve her credit card. "No. I think I have everything."

Alex caught a glimpse of a photograph of John that confirmed that this was indeed the Lorraine he was married to. She forced a smile and her throat constricted as she bagged the other accessories and handed the woman back the card. "Thanks for coming in. Have a nice day."

"You too."

All the fantasies that Alex allowed herself to entertain with regard to John seemed to sashay out the door with his wife. Knowing that he was married was one thing. Putting a face to the life he had outside of protecting hers was quite another.

An hour later Alex's coworker Margot returned. "Sorry that took me a little longer than I thought it was going to. Did Celeste ever come in?"

"Not yet," Alex responded.

"Did Mrs. Chase come by?"

"Yes. She did indeed."

"There wasn't a problem was there?"

"No. No problem. She came in, got her order, bought some other pieces, and left."

"Other than that has it been very busy?"

"Nothing that I couldn't handle."

The woman slurped the rest of her drink from its container before tossing it into a trash can behind the register. Alex finished folding a stack of assorted cashmere sweaters and announced that she would be taking her break.

"Oh, Adriane, before you go, I almost forgot to ask. What are you doing tonight?"

"No big plans," Alex responded. "Why?"

"There's this new club that just opened in North Hollywood that I've been dying to go to. Are you interested in coming with?"

"No. I'm not really the club type."

Margot cocked her head coyly. "Seriously, because you seem like a lot of fun."

"Well, I'm not ready for a retirement home or anything, but I do have other responsibilities."

"You mean your kid?"

"Yeah," Alex responded. "I like spending time with . . . my kid."

"Aw, c'mon. It's Thursday and you're off tomorrow. When's the last time you let your hair down and let yourself go?"

"I don't know, Margot. I don't really feel like letting myself go."

"Oh, I get it. There's a guy, right?"

"No, there's no guy."

"Then c'mon, it'll be fun. Who knows, maybe you'll meet a guy. Hell, maybe you'll meet more than one."

Alex thought about what her mother said, and everything she'd been feeling for John, and coming face to face with Lorraine Chase, and decided to take the woman up on her offer. "Okay . . . fine. I'll go."

"Great. I promise you'll have a good time."

"But, I'm driving my own car. That way I can leave when I want to."

"Absolutely. I don't have a problem meeting you there."

"What's the name of this place anyway?"

"It's called Bricks."

"It's not a gay bar is it?"

"No. Of course not." Margot flicked her French-tipped nails through the spiky fringe of her coif. "Oh, wait . . . do you think I'm a lesbian?"

"No, Margot, I don't think you're a lesbian."

"Good. Because I can promise you that nothing makes me happier than a good stiff cock . . . tail." She laughed. "I just thought you might want to hang out, that's all."

Alex smiled. "I haven't had a good stiff one in a long time. Sounds like just what I need."

Alex swept her hair into an up-do, allowing a few loose tendrils to cascade down the side of her face and neck. For the first time in a long time she felt a little lighthearted as she found a revealing strapless black and silver micro mini designer original hanging in the back of her closet that she'd all but forgotten she had from her former life. The last time she'd worn it was for a party she planned for a hip-hop mogul back in Atlanta. Fortunately, she hadn't held on to any baby weight, so she was able to shimmy seamlessly into it and back into the remnants of the old Alex again: vivacious, sexy, and desirable. She rechecked her makeup and spritzed on Desire before sliding into a pair of stilettos that accentuated her legs to complete the look.

"Well, now, Cerena will you get a look at your mother." Jamilah beamed as she entered Alex's room. "You look amazing, daughter."

Alex smiled as she checked herself out in the mirror. "I feel amazing, Mama. I remember this woman."

"As do I."

"Are you sure you don't mind taking care of Cerena tonight?"

"Not at all. I'm going over to Ernie Mae's with the rest of the girls to play cards. This little one will more than likely be out like a light by seven or so."

"Well, if anything happens you call me and I'll come right back."

"Nothing is going to happen. We'll be fine. You just go on and have a good time."

Alex grabbed her clutch and wrap and kissed her mother's cheek and then kissed Cerena. "Thanks, Mama. I won't be out that late."

"Don't worry about anything here. Stay out for as long as you like."

Bricks was among the flashiest nightclubs in the San Fernando Valley area that dotted Lankershim Boulevard in North Hollywood (NoHo as it was referred to by the locals). Like most new hot spots it had quickly become the happening place to be. Alex navigated up to her place in the line of cars and waited for the valet; the velvet rope, the beefy bouncers at the door, the air of celebrity all reminded her of grander days. Once she entered the club she wandered around looking for Margot, who had promised to be waiting near the door at the designated time. She wasn't.

Alex made her way to the bar. "I'll have Grey Goose with a twist of lime."

"I gotcha." The bartender winked and smiled.

One of the best things about bars in California was that smoking was prohibited. Alex had no worry about going home smelling like an ashtray. Just as she got her drink and took a sip she heard her name being screamed through the crowd over the volume of music.

"Adriane!"

She turned and saw Margot pushing through and headed toward her, dragging a man behind her who could have been a Ryan Gosling lookalike. "Sorry I'm late. Traffic was so backed up on the 134. Damn, girl, you look great," Margot shrieked. "I love that dress. You look totally hot!"

Alex smiled. "Thanks."

"For somebody who doesn't go to clubs you sure know how to pull it together."

The man standing with her smiled salaciously. "Margot, aren't you going to introduce me to your friend?"

"Oh, yeah, Zach, this is Adriane. She's the one I was telling you about. She thought I was a lesbiiiiaan."

Judging by the slur of her words it appeared that Margot already had a drink or two.

Alex ignored her comment and extended her hand to the man. "Nice to meet you, Zach."

"Nice to meet you too." The man held on to Alex's hand a little too long. She was uncomfortable feeling his index finger massaging her palm, and wrested it away.

Margot leaned in closer to her. "Hey . . . you want a bump?"

"A bump?"

"Coke. You want some?"

Alex shook her head. "No. I'll pass."

"C'mon . . . this is some really quality shit."

"I don't think so."

The man caressed Alex's bare shoulder. "You don't know what you're missin'."

Alex pulled away. "I have some idea, and I'm not interested."

"I think Zach likes you," Margot cooed. "We should really have some fun. Have you ever been part of a ménage à trois?"

Alex chuckled. The irony of Margot's enticement wasn't lost considering her prior denouncement of being a lesbian. She was no prude. In another life she had been a little more sexually uninhibited. But she didn't think getting it on with a coworker and her movie idol–looking boyfriend was the sort of thing Adriane should be doing. "Why don't you guys go ahead. I'll sit this one out."

"Suit yourself. C'mon, Zach, let's dance."

As Alex watched the two go off to the dance floor she thought that it was funny how you really don't get to know the people you work with until you see them in a social setting.

"Friends of yours?" the bartender queried.

"Um . . . 'friends' is debatable." Alex laughed again.

The bartender turned to tend to other customers and Alex curiously continued to check out the crowd. David Guetta and Akon's aptly titled "Sexy Bitch" reverberated through the club and sent the revelers into a frenzy of twisting and sexually energized thrusts. A few minutes later the bartender returned and set another drink down in front of Alex.

"Courtesy of the gentleman at the end of the bar," he noted.

Alex glanced down the length of the bar and as the strobe lights flashed across the man's face and reflected off the mirrored walls she was stunned to see who she thought was Xavier Rivera raising his glass to her. Clearly spooked, she jumped off the stool, not looking back, and bolted for the exit. The more people who crowded in on her the more claustrophobic she felt as she frantically pushed through. She couldn't get to the door fast enough. When she got outside she got the attention of one of the bouncers.

"Lady, what is it?"

"Please, you have to help me. There's a man in there who wants to kill me."

"What?"

Alex instantly realized how insane she sounded. The brawny bouncer moved her aside and looked through the throng of people passing into the club. Alex's hands shook as she rifled through her bag to find the parking ticket for her car to give to the valet.

"Are you sure there's somebody after you?" the bouncer asked. "You're not high on somethin' are you?"

"No, I'm not high dammit. I know what I saw," Alex responded. "Please. I just need to get out of here."

The valet ran to get her car while she waited, cowering behind a man as thick as a linebacker. When the valet finally pulled up Alex jumped in and sped off without offering a tip.

It felt like she couldn't breathe from the time she left North Hollywood until she pulled up at her house in Monrovia. No one had followed her. It was just after nine-thirty and the street was quiet. She exited the car and bolted into the house. Neither Jamilah nor the baby was there. She looked across the street to see that the lights were on at the Hudson house and surmised that Jamilah must still be there playing cards. She called her up to be sure, calming herself before she spoke.

"Hi, Mama . . . No . . . No . . . I just got home. I had a headache and the club was just too loud. Is everything okay over there? Cerena is sleeping. Good. No. Take your time. Have fun." After speaking to Jamilah she instinctively dialed John but hung up before it rang. She took a deep breath and lay back on the sofa. "It wasn't Rivera. It couldn't have been him."

6

Dresses lay crumpled on the dressing room floor of Lorraine Chase's large walk-in closet. Shoes were scattered haphazardly. She felt as nervous as she did the first time John asked her out. She needed for everything to fall into place tonight if she planned on seducing him back into their bed. It was silly, she thought, trying to capitalize on her daughter's moment. After all, how romantic could the sight of twelve five-year-old girls prancing around on stage in tulle and crinoline be? She had to find the right look that wouldn't make her appear too eager. Her seduction should be pointed, but subtle. John was no fool. After changing more times than a runway model she tried on a form-hugging skirt and blouse with a plunging neckline, but it was going to take more than revealing cleavage to win him over. The only real weapons in her arsenal were their children. He would do anything for them; that much she was sure of.

Chloe stood excitedly at the window, waiting to see her father's truck. "Mommy, come on," she squealed.

John pulled into the driveway and Chloe dashed out to meet him. He hoisted her in his arms and kissed her. "You guys ready?"

He looked up and saw Lorraine at the door. She'd settled on a less obvious skirt and a lightweight knit sweater that accentuated the blue in her eyes.

"Did you get the camcorder?"

She held it up. "I got it right here."

"Where's John Michael?"

"I'm coming," the boy shouted as he bounded down the steps with little thought to his broken arm.

"Slow down, John Michael," Lorraine cautioned him. She handed the camcorder to John and turned to lock up the house. "Do you want to take the Jag?"

"I wanna ride in Dad's truck," John Michael insisted.

"Me too," Chloe chimed in.

"There's room," John said. "Why don't we all ride together?"

Lorraine nodded agreeably. As far as she was concerned, as long as they were in the same space they could have taken public transportation to the school.

Once they made it to the auditorium Chloe found her teacher and the other girls and dashed off to get ready. Lorraine carried her head a little bit higher as she and John strolled inside. She smiled and waved at the other mothers she was sure had been cattily discussing the state of her union behind her back. If she could have reached out to take John's arm to show their solidarity she would have.

Barbara Mitchell, John's mother, was already seated when she noticed him and John Michael. Her youthful countenance and shapely figure gave little away of her fifty-plus years. Her eyes lit up and she waved, signaling that she'd saved seats for them. They exchanged hugs before settling in. Barbara glanced over at Lorraine, nodded, and smiled disdainfully. It was the kind of interaction that only a mother would give to the woman who had hurt her son.

The conversational chatter in the auditorium hushed twenty minutes later when the lights dimmed. The overture rose from the orchestra pit and Lorraine settled back, basking in her small triumph as the curtain went up. Chloe may have been the lead of Becket Academy's presentation of *Swan Lake,* but it was Lorraine's performance that would win the day . . . with everyone except her disapproving mother-in-law.

After the show John took them all out for ice cream; his mother chose not to go. Despite that, he and Lorraine found common ground as they raved about Chloe's dancing. By the end of the night Chloe had worn herself out and fell asleep on the way home. John carried her up to bed while Lorraine saw to John Michael. When John came back downstairs Lorraine had taken the liberty of fixing him a drink.

"I should be going."

"It's only a little after nine," Lorraine said. "Can't you at least have one drink with me?"

John scratched his forehead and took the glass.

"To our prima ballerina," Lorraine toasted.

"All those dancing lessons paid off." John laughed. "At least she knows stage right from stage left, which is more than I can say for the Thompsons' kid."

They both laughed. Lorraine casually poured more brandy into John's glass. He didn't object. "Thank you for recording tonight. Mom and Dad would really be upset if they didn't get a chance to see Chloe's debut."

"Are they still in Belize?"

"They should be back tomorrow."

John nodded and tossed back the brandy. Lorraine seized the opportunity to make a move. Her fingers delicately traced his brow and down the side of his face and she kissed him. His reaction wasn't immediate. It wasn't until she tugged at the buttons of his shirt that he moved away.

He shook his head. "Lorraine, don't."

"You still want me. I know you do." She stepped back in front of him and stared into his eyes. The room was still and thick with tension. The light was dim. There were yet unresolved emotions that had not been dealt with and they both felt it. Her fingers caressed his lips and he yielded to her, promptly pulling her sweater up over her head and kissing her neck and lips and face. She threw her head back in ecstasy and nimbly undid the buckle of his belt. His breathing grew more intense as she massaged his erect penis. She slowly sank to her knees and took its fullness into her mouth. He gasped and quivered. After a few seconds, as if snapping out of a trance, he pushed her away.

"Stop," he insisted.

"You don't want me to. I know you don't." Ignoring his protest she skillfully sucked his erection back into her mouth.

"Mommy, my stomach hurts."

John and Lorraine jumped in tandem. He pulled away and stumbled backward as he yanked his pants back up and fumbled with the buttons on his shirt.

Lorraine stood, grabbed her sweater, and wiped the corners of her mouth with her index finger and thumb. "Chloe, sweetie, don't come downstairs; Mommy's coming up."

John cleared his throat. "I should go."

"No, wait. Just give me a minute."

"We can't do this, Lorraine."

"Mommy."

Lorraine's look implored him to stay.

He nodded toward the staircase. "Go ahead, Chloe needs you." He grabbed his keys from the bar and swiftly left the house.

"Mommy."

Lorraine smiled and teared up simultaneously. There was the tiniest crack in the façade. His body responded and she felt, if given the time, she would have had his heart again as well. "I'm coming, baby."

John sat in his truck, thinking about what just happened. He looked down at his flaccid penis and shook his head. "Boy, you need to calm that shit down. You were about to get me into some serious trouble." He glanced back up toward the house before driving off, and exhaled.

John woke up the next morning beating himself up for allowing things to get so out of hand with Lorraine the previous night. He sat up on the side of his bed and contemplated calling Alex but guilt changed his mind. He pulled at his boxers and went to the bathroom to relieve himself. He then plodded barefoot into the kitchen, scratching his chest as he slipped into a T-shirt. He looked into the refrigerator for something to eat and started a pot of coffee. As the coffee brewed he checked his brother's room to see if he was asleep, and discovered that he wasn't there. A knock drew his attention to the door.

"Hank, what are you doin' here?"

"Good mornin' to you too."

"Sorry, it's early. Come on in."

"I was on my way to the pier to do some fishin' and your mother wanted me to stop by and bring this extra lasagna she made. She was sure you and your brother were up here livin' off In-N-Out Burger and Pizza Hut."

"You detoured up here from Inglewood on your way to the pier to bring me lasagna?"

"You know your mother."

"She was tryin' to be slick." John took the lasagna into the kitchen, dug a spoonful out, and shoved it into his mouth. "She just wanted to know if I was home and if I was alone."

"You figured that out, did you?"

"It didn't take a whole lot of effort after last night."

Hank laughed. "You know your mother told me that Lorraine was actin' all cozy with you."

"Yep, that's the reason for the lasagna and the unannounced visit, right?"

"Sorry I didn't get to make it last night. Your mother showed me all the pictures though."

"Yeah, Chloe did her thing."

Hank glanced around the unkempt bachelor's lair. "Is that fresh coffee I smell?"

"Yeah. Want some?"

"Sure, just as long as the cup's clean."

"Huh?" John looked through the portal separating the kitchen from the living room to see his stepfather pushing aside a pile of clothes from one end of the sofa in order to sit. "Sorry about the mess. I've been meaning to straighten up, just haven't had the time. You want cream and sugar?"

"No, just black."

"When did you start drinking black coffee?"

"When your mother decided that I needed to cut back. It's an acquired taste."

John chuckled as he grabbed two mismatched mugs from the cupboard and filled them. He went back into the living room, gave his imposing and distinguished stepfather one, and sat in a chair facing him.

"Where's Anthony?"

"I don't know. He wasn't here when I came in last night and he wasn't here when I got up this morning. Probably spent the night with some woman."

"Speaking of women, what's goin' on with you and Lorraine?"

"Nothin', but that hasn't stopped her from wanting to get back together."

"I take it you don't want to?"

"It's complicated."

Hank scratched at the grayed temples of his faded haircut and took a sip of his coffee. "Complicated, huh? Sounds like there's another woman."

"What would make you say that?"

"Look, I'm almost sixty-three years old, and if I ain't learned nothin' else in all this time I know that nothin' can complicate a situation between a man and a woman more than another woman." Hank's dark brow furrowed. "Unless it's another man."

John caught his meaning. "Hell, no. Not up in here." He pressed his lips together and stared off. "To be honest with you there is this woman."

"Is she married?"

John exhaled. "No. She's uh . . . she's in the program."

"Aw, hell. You gotta be kiddin' me."

"I didn't plan on it. I didn't expect it. It just sort of happened."

"Johnny . . ." Hank scratched his head again and planted his face in his large, calloused hand.

"I know what you're gonna say, Hank. Believe me it's nothing I haven't said to myself over and over again."

"You have feelings for this woman?"

John put his cup down on the table in front of him and vigorously rubbed his face. "Yeah . . . God help me I do."

"Walk away, son," Hank admonished. "Maybe you should concentrate on some of your other cases. No good can come of the situation with this woman."

"I have to finish the job I started. She's counting on me."

"Johnny, I can't tell you how to feel. You've always been as stubborn as your mother. And you always did like the rush of livin' on the edge. But, are you sure this woman is worth you puttin' everything on the line you've worked so hard for? Have you thought about passin' this one off on somebody else?"

"Yeah, I thought about it."

"But you're not doin' anything to change it? This must be one helluva woman."

John retreated to his bedroom, and when he reemerged he passed Hank a picture of Alex.

Hank removed his eyeglasses from the inside pocket of his skiff jacket and slid them up his nose. "Is this her?"

"Yeah."

"Don't tell me you sleep with this under your pillow."

John snatched the picture back. "Not funny, man."

"She's good-lookin', that's for sure. I can see why you might be tempted."

"And that's not even a good picture of her. Man, this woman is somethin' else. There's just something . . . I can't really explain how I feel when I'm around her."

"So, it's more than sex then?"

"I haven't slept with her."

"Are you going to?"

John shook his head. "I don't know what I'm gonna do."

"Is it the danger of being with this woman that appeals to you?"

John shrugged his shoulders. "Maybe."

"You need to figure it out, son, and soon. I think what you need is to step away for a minute and get a fresh perspective. How about a drive to Santa Monica? We can do some fishin' and you can do some thinkin'?"

"I can't today."

Hank stood up and his six foot four inch frame towered over John, making him feel like that hapless fourteen-year-old again. "All right. Watch your step. I don't want your mother throwin' another fit because of another woman she thinks you're ruining your life over."

"You can't say anything to her about this, Hank."

"Don't worry, I won't. But if this thing with this woman blows up, your mother and her prayer group are gonna be draggin' your tail to the altar and drowning you in holy oil."

Even though he laughed John knew Hank was right. As much as Barbara Mitchell resented Lorraine for what she'd done she tolerated her for the sake of the grandchildren. His involvement with Alex would carry no such amnesty.

7

Jamilah sat on a bench in a neighborhood park, reading and soaking in the afternoon sun, rocking Cerena back and forth in her stroller. She lowered her reading glasses and smiled as she spied the older gentlemen she'd met in the market approaching. He smiled too.

"I was hoping to find you here."

"How are you, Mr. Obafemi?"

"Ah, ah, ah . . . Please, call me Ade."

Jamilah nodded politely. "How are you today, Ade?"

"I am much better now that I'm seeing you."

Jamilah's eyes smiled as she readjusted on the bench to allow the man to sit. He removed his cap and his sponge of white hair sprung up from beneath it. He sat, boyishly twirling the cap in his hand as if wanting to say something but not sure how to begin.

"What are you reading?"

Jamilah turned the cover of the book over to show him. "It's a collection of poetry by Phillis Wheatley."

He looked off in the distance. "My Busola loved poetry. She was a schoolteacher, you know."

"Is that right?"

"I used to love for her to read to me. Her voice was so calming. Much like yours."

"Thank you." Jamilah smiled amiably, closed her eyes, and turned her face upward toward the radiance of the sun. "It is a beautiful day."

"Yes, it is very nice," Ade responded. "Your granddaughter seems to be taking advantage of the time to have a nap."

"You should be glad she's sleeping, otherwise, she would be trying to talk your ears off."

"I would welcome the conversation. How old did you say she was?"

"She'll be nine months this May. She started taking her first steps just recently."

"You must be very proud."

"Yes, I am."

"I have a two-year-old grandson who I have not seen since he was born, but my daughter sends pictures." Ade gazed off over the park. "I miss my family very much. My daughter and son-in-law have tried many times since my wife died to get me to move to Chicago to live with them."

"Why didn't you go?"

"Because my Busola is buried here, and I wanted to stay close to her."

"I understand."

Ade cleared his throat and turned back to Jamilah. "Would you mind terribly reading something to me from your book?"

Jamilah girlishly brushed the loose strands of silver behind her ears and leafed through her book for an appropriate passage.

O Thou bright jewel in my aim I strive
To comprehend thee. Thine own words declare
Wisdom is higher than a fool can reach.
I cease to wonder, and no more attempt
Thine height t' explore, or fathom thy profound.
But, O my soul, sink not into despair,
Virtue is near thee, and with gentle hand
Would now embrace thee, hovers o'er thine head.
Fain would the heav'n-born soul with her converse,
Then seek, then court her for her promis'd bliss.

Ade turned to her as if he'd summoned the courage to ask what it seemed he'd wanted to all along. "Miss Janette, I would be most honored if you were to join me for dinner tomorrow night."

Jamilah sat contemplating the invitation. She hadn't had a suitor in quite some time. He was alone and so was she. They were both from Nigeria and appeared to have a lot in common despite the fact that he was almost ten years her senior. She welcomed the companionship and why shouldn't she? With the exception of the three elderly women she met with on occasion to play bid whist, all the friendships she'd cultivated over the years were now dissolved back in boroughs of the Bronx. There was no telling what was made of her disappearance. And there was absolutely no reason she couldn't try to make the best of this fortuitous encounter.

"Ade, I would like very much to have dinner with you."

"Where would you like to go?"

"Where would you like to take me?"

"Well, there is a very nice restaurant not too far from here. The Café Mundial. Have you been there?"

"No, I haven't as yet."

"I have a car. I could pick you up. Is six o'clock too early?"

"My daughter has to work. I don't think she will get home until seven."

"Then shall we say seven-thirty?"

"That sounds lovely."

Jamilah's acceptance seemed to put Ade at ease. He leaned back on the bench and she opened her book and found another sonnet to read to him. He closed his eyes and was quieted by the warmth of her voice.

8

It was nearing closing time at La Bella. Other than a few words about various business transactions, Margot had done her best to avoid conversing with Alex for most of the day; which had not gone unnoticed by Celeste, the silver-haired, cosmetically enhanced trendsetter who owned the boutique. She cornered Margot in the stockroom when she went to collect her purse from her locker.

"Margot, are you feeling all right?"

"Yes. I'm fine. Why do you ask?"

"You've not been your usually bubbly self today, that's all. There seems to be quite a bit of tension between you and Adriane. Is there anything going on that I need to know about?"

"No. Everything's fine. Do you need me to hang around until you lock up?"

"It's all right. I'll take care of it."

The two women emerged from the back room as Alex was headed for the door.

Celeste waved. "Good night, Adriane."

"Good night, Celeste. I'll see you in the morning."

Margot hurried to catch up to Alex as she stepped out onto the sidewalk. "Adriane, wait up."

Alex stopped and turned toward her.

Margot fidgeted with her chunky necklace. "I, uh, I wanted to . . . I wanted to apologize for the other night. After I thought about it I felt so embarrassed about the way I acted. I thought that you might have said something to Celeste. I really can't afford to lose this job."

"You don't have to worry about anything like that with me. What you do when you're not at work is your business. I thought you were giving me shade all day because I skipped out."

"That's funny," Margot responded. "I thought you left because of the things I said to you."

"I'm a big girl, Margot. Why don't we just chalk this up to miscommunication and leave it at that?"

"That works for me. Thanks for being so cool about it. So, I'll see you tomorrow then?"

Alex nodded and proceeded to her car. She was surprised to find John waiting for her there. "Two Chases in one week," Alex scoffed. "I must've hit the lottery."

John's brow furrowed at Alex's sardonic comment. "What do you mean two Chases?"

"Your wife was here shopping a couple of days ago."

"Lorraine?"

"Unless you have another one hidden away somewhere. Petite, red hair, blue eyes. I have to say she was not quite what I expected."

"You mean because she's white."

"It does seem to play into every stereotype I ever heard, a good-looking black man, a perky white trophy wife."

John flashed back on what had transpired between him and Lorraine in the middle of the living room floor. He thought he could push the incident down somewhere in the recesses of his mind, where such things are more surreal than reality.

"Is something wrong?"

"Huh?"

"Why are you here, John?" Alex looked upward into the sky. "No Bat-Signal. So, feel free to take the night off."

"Maybe I'm not here to protect you. Maybe I need you to protect me this time."

"From what exactly?"

"Myself. I'm afraid that not seeing you every day makes me feel a little bit crazy."

"Oh, please."

"Yeah, I know. That didn't sound as lame in my head."

"Then maybe that's where it should've stayed," Alex responded.

John smiled mannishly. "You're not going to cut me any slack, are you?"

"Should I?"

"I was hoping you would. I thought I might hear from you yesterday. I kinda got used to worrying about you."

"I thought this was a rescue mission to save you."

"It is. You could save me from eating alone if you would agree to have dinner with me."

Alex sighed. "It's been a long day. I need to get home."

"Do you want company?"

"I was trying to make a conscious effort to give you your space, John. Keeping whatever this is as professional as possible."

"How's that workin' for you?"

"Apparently about as well as it is for you."

"Look, I can't stop thinking about you. I know what I'm opening myself up to, but the bottom line is I'm attracted to you."

Alex sidestepped him and tried to open the door to her car. He grabbed her arm and pulled her back toward him. "I'm not going to let you jump in your car and go speeding off again, leaving me standing here to pick up my pride. I'm not going to press the issue either."

"Have you been drinking?"

"I had a few beers with my brother."

"Needed a little liquid courage?"

John sighed and rubbed his hand over his head and face. "Well, I'm not blaming it on the alcohol."

"Cute." Alex smirked.

"Maybe it's the full moon," John countered. "Maybe I just need to be straight up with you. Now, we can either be adults about it, or you can be childish. I thought you were more woman than that. Was I wrong?"

Alex cut her eyes and huffed. "You apparently don't know me as well as you think you do. I'm a lot more woman than you can handle, Inspector."

"Then prove it."

Alex tossed her purse onto the hood of her car, traced her fingers over the outline of his broad shoulders and the veins that popped from his muscular arms protruding from his T-shirt. She licked her lips seductively as her hands stroked his chest, and she pressed her body into his, fondling his hardening erection.

"So, is that a yes to the company?"

"I haven't made up my mind yet," she whispered.

John leaned in and kissed her. Long. Hard. Passionate. "Does that help?"

"Are you sure you want to do this, John?"

"I know that I've wanted to do that for a very long time."

"What about—"

He pressed his mouth onto hers again. "I think that if we don't go somewhere fast I'm going to take you in the bed of my truck and show you just how hard it's been for me to keep this thing professional."

"I didn't think you were that kinky."

"You don't believe me?" He pulled at the hem of her skirt to assert his claim and she slapped it away.

"Okay, okay. Why don't you come over to the house . . . for dinner?"

"Oh, yeah, I wanna eat, but what I have in mind I don't think we should be doing in front of your mother."

"Then it's a good thing that Mama's going out with friends tonight."

"I'll meet you back at your house."

Alex exhaled as she drove away from the boutique and watched John following her from the rearview mirror. She was prepared to throw caution to the wind and give herself wholly to the temptation that had been courting her for months.

When she arrived home she was startled by the sight of a strange man in her living room. Ade courteously stood up, nodded to her, and straightened his tie.

"You must be Janette's daughter." He extended his hand.

"Yes, I am."

"I can see that you are just as lovely as your mother."

"Where exactly is my mother?"

"She's getting dressed."

"I'm sorry. Who are you?"

"Ade Obafemi."

"Here you are, Omolola."

Alex turned with a puzzled expression on her face.

"I see you've met Ade."

"Mama, I assumed when you said you were going to dinner it was with one of the ladies down the street."

"Why would you assume that, Omolola?"

John stepped in behind Alex and interrupted an uncomfortable moment.

"I thought we'd settled this," Jamilah continued.

"I didn't mean that, Mama."

John shifted his gaze between the two women and then looked at Ade suspiciously.

"Ade Obafemi," he said, extending his hand to John.

"John Chase."

"Mama, can I talk to you for a minute?"

Jamilah glanced at Ade, who smiled and nodded. She then followed Alex to her bedroom.

"Before you say anything, Ade is a nice man," Jamilah started.

"He's the man you met at the market?"

"Yes," Jamilah huffed. "He's the widower. He's from Nigeria. He's been in this country for twelve years. He has two children, a son who still lives in Abuja, and a daughter who lives in Chicago."

Alex brushed her hand over her mouth. "Mama."

"Do you want his social security number and blood type, too, or is that enough information for you?" Jamilah snapped. "He's lonely just like me, and we're just going to have dinner."

An awkward silence seeped between them.

"I'm sorry, Mama. I know you're lonely. I'm sorry I made you feel like you were being interrogated. I don't have the right to dictate who you can go out with."

"I'm glad you understand that, daughter."

"If you say he's a good guy I trust your instincts."

Jamilah opened her arms and Alex melted into her embrace. "Thank you, Omolola."

"So, where is Mr. Obafemi taking you?"

"The Café Mundial."

"That's a nice restaurant."

"I should probably get back in there before John drives him off. Cerena's been fed. I put her down about an hour ago."

"Thank you, Mama. You go. Have a good time."

"I will."

As their roles reversed, Alex stood at the door and watched Jamilah ride off with her date. John walked up behind her and wrapped his arms around her waist.

"I sent a text to Harley and asked him to run a check on your mother's friend."

"Am I crazy to be concerned?"

"No. You're not." John swept the hair away from Alex's neck and licked and kissed it.

"What are you doing?"

"Picking up where we left off."

He pulled her back into the house and closed the door. His mouth found hers and their tongues and lips fervently intermingled. She yanked at his T-shirt and pulled it over his head. His heartbeat kept time with her intensified breathing. They continued to kiss and giggle like horny teenagers, bumping into walls as she led him to her room.

"Shhhh," she cautioned him. "Don't wake the baby."

He teetered from one foot to the other, kicking off shoes and quickly shedding his jeans and socks.

"Well, that answers that question," Alex teased.

"What question is that?"

"Whether you wore boxers or briefs."

"I could show you something that these boxers can't contain."

"I can already see that, too."

He removed his watch and laid it on the bureau and grabbed her and spun her around. She released a small yelp and pressed into his groin. His large hands gently caressed her stomach and cupped her breasts, kneading them like putty. She moaned appreciatively as he brushed his face over the curve and nape of her neck, simultaneously sliding the straps of her camisole off her shoulders. He backed up slightly, taking his time unzipping her skirt, and pushed it away from her hips. He ran his hands seductively down her body, and slid her panties down far enough to allow his fingers ample access to massage her clitoris. Alex threw her head back and moaned as his exploration took on a life of its own. Her legs trembled. She backed up into the wall for balance, nearly knocking down a framed picture as he kissed and licked a trail over her body, until his lips and tongue came to suck the upper part of her fleshy thighs.

"Oh shit," she sighed.

He licked and tongued his way into the most sensitive recesses of her vaginal walls until she shuddered into orgasm, grabbing his bald head and pulling it closer into her.

"Shit! Shit!" she moaned.

He wriggled free of his boxers and his penis danced buoyantly between his legs as he crouched back down to finish what he'd begun. She pulled her hair and held her breath to stifle a scream as another orgasm burned through her. They were jarred by the ringing vibration of his cell phone.

"Don't answer it," she pleaded.

"It could be about the guy your mother is with."

John pulled away and finagled his phone from the pocket of his jeans. He looked back at Alex and winked as he licked her juices from his fingers. Breathlessly, Alex peeled herself off the wall, ambled over to the bed, and lay back, waiting as he read the text. "What did it say?"

"Apparently Ade Obafemi seems to be exactly who he says he is. He has a son in Nigeria. Daughter in Chicago. Your mother is in good hands." He removed a condom from his pocket, tossed the phone onto the pile of clothes on the floor, then climbed on the bed between her legs. "And so are you."

"If I ever doubted it before I don't anymore, Inspector."

He extracted the condom from its packet and teased her with a look as he rolled it on. "I want you so damn much."

Alex coquettishly spread her legs farther apart. "Then what are you waiting for? Bon appétit."

John lowered himself on top of her and smothered her with tender kisses as he worked his manhood into position. He rose up and balanced on the palms of his hands, purposefully staring into her eyes. His hungry penis glided over her wet hole, teasing it into submission until it seemed to scream for his entry. He slowly worked his way inside inch by delicious inch. She gasped and quivered, accepting all of him. He was deliberate and methodical, rhythmic, thrusting only fast enough to teeter on the brink of ejaculation and then pulling out and reentering. It was slow, sweet torture. Alex clawed at his back and dug her nails into his butt cheeks as she came again. Finally, he launched into a fevered pitch. His loins tightened and his tempo quickened. There was no more holding back.

"Damn," he shouted, burying his face into the pillow under her head. "Fuck!" He rolled over and dropped to her side, laughing.

"What's so funny?"

"That was one of the best damn dinners I ever had."

She pulled up and straddled him. "There's plenty more where that came from."

"Give me a minute to catch my breath, woman."

She ran her hand over the perspiration on his chest, kissed him, and laid her head down.

"You know, I just thought of something."

"What?"

"Do you think your mother is havin' this much fun with Ade?"

Alex rose up and popped John on the side of his head. "That's not funny."

He sat up and pulled her back to him. "I'm sorry, baby. I didn't mean anything by it. You forgive me?"

"I know it's crazy, but it's hard enough for me to think about her with anybody but my father."

"Your mother is a beautiful, vibrant woman. Any man would be a fool not to see that. It's not as if she's cheating on your father. Not like . . ."

"Not like what?"

"Never mind. Forget it."

Alex pulled herself up and looked at him. "No . . . finish what you were about to say. Not like what?"

John blew a disgusted breath. "Not like Lorraine did with me."

"Are you serious?"

"Now is not exactly the time to be talking about this."

Alex smiled and ran a manicured fingernail across the base of his neck. "You said you needed a minute, right?"

John rubbed his head and lay back against the pillows. "The whole thing was partially my fault, with the job and all. I've hardly been there for her or the kids."

"So, she dealt with that by sleeping with another man?"

"She was screwing some guy she met at the gym months before we separated. She was sharing our personal business and they were getting closer while we were drifting apart."

"How did you find out?"

"I accidentally picked up the extension in the house one day and heard the two of them on the phone making plans to meet. I followed her to his place and I saw them together."

"What did you do?"

"It shocked the shit out of me. I didn't know what to do. I didn't confront her about it . . . not right away. I was angry enough to kill both of 'em, but I wasn't about to get into an OJ situation, you know what I mean. So, I drove home and waited for her. She cried and begged me to forgive her. We even tried counseling, but it was never going to be the same between us after that. I tried. But once trust is broken it takes a helluva lot to get it back."

"Yeah, I guess you're right."

John sat up and leaned back on the headboard. "This changes everything between us, you know that, right?"

Alex readjusted accordingly. "Yeah."

"But I'm not sorry we did it." He reached out and caressed Alex's backside.

She leaned in and kissed him. "Me either."

"You better stop before you get me up again."

"I thought that was the objective," she teased.

"You wouldn't want your mother walking in on us, would you?"

Alex glanced at the clock on her nightstand and laughed. "No, that wouldn't be a good thing to have happen at all."

"We should probably get dressed."

They got out of bed and Alex slipped into her robe and went to the linen closet for a towel. When she came back to the room she leaned against the doorjamb and watched John's naked form from behind as he peered out the window. "Damn, I feel like singin' that Salt-n-Pepa song right now."

He turned away from the window and strode over to her, smiling. "Oh yeah, what song would that be?"

"'You're packed and you're stacked 'specially in the back. Brother, wanna thank your mother for a butt like that.'"

John grabbed hold of Alex's rear and laughed. "Your mother didn't do such a bad job herself."

He kissed her and slid her robe off her shoulders. She squirmed free, pulled it back up, and tossed him the towel.

"You just gon' leave me hangin'?"

"For now."

"Okay, I see how you are."

John stepped into the bathroom and Alex picked his T-shirt off the floor and held it to her nose, inhaling his scent. She looked down and saw that his cell phone was vibrating and picked it up. She smirked when she read Lorraine's name on the caller ID.

A few minutes later when he came out of the bathroom he found Alex lounging on the bed, draped in his T-shirt.

"Your wife called. I didn't answer it, but I have to admit I was tempted for about half a second."

"So, what stopped you?"

"Didn't feel like being malicious."

He pulled on his boxer shorts and jeans and held out his hand to her. "Can I have my shirt, please?"

She slowly pulled it over her head and helped him by pulling it over his.

"I won't be washing this shirt anytime soon." He picked up his cell phone and noted the message indicator on the phone. "Lorraine apparently called more than once."

"I guess we were too busy to notice," Alex said, slipping her robe back on.

"I should go." He took her by the hand and led her out of the room to the front of the house. "I'll have to take a rain check on that dinner."

"I wasn't that hungry anyway."

He smiled. "I wasn't talking about food."

They embraced and kissed again and then she watched him as he sauntered out to his truck. She closed the door and fell against it with a satisfied purr. After checking on her daughter she cleaned herself up and put her room back in order. She then went to the kitchen for a glass of juice.

It was after ten and Jamilah still had not made it in. Alex stared out the window as if expecting to see them pulling up in the driveway, and dismissed the feeling that something might be wrong.

She sat down on the sofa, turned on the television and flipped listlessly through the channels. Anxiety washed over her as it neared eleven o'clock. She shut off the television and dialed Jamilah's cell phone; it rang straight to voicemail. She grabbed the telephone book.

"What was the name of that restaurant? Café? Café? Here it is. Café Mundial."

She dialed. There was no answer. She tried again.

"Café Mundial. May I help you?"

"Um, hello. I was calling to see if you could tell me if a particular couple was there having dinner tonight?"

"Sorry. We're closed," responded the female on the other end of the line.

"Okay, but maybe you saw the people I'm looking for."

"I'm sorry, Miss. I don't think I can help you. There were a lot of people in and out of here tonight."

"Please. This is extremely important. It's a matter of life and death."

She could hear the woman's annoyance. "Okay, what do you need?"

"Hopefully you saw a black woman in her mid-fifties come in tonight with an older, distinguished-looking black man with all-white hair."

"I don't really recall anyone like that."

"Please. The woman would have had medium-length salt-and-pepper hair. She was wearing uh . . . uh . . . a purple silk blouse with a beige skirt."

"I'm sorry. It would be impossible for me to tell you that."

"Well, can I speak to your manager? Hello . . . Hello."

The line went dead.

Alex threw the phone up against the wall. "Dammit!" The fierce clanging noise woke Cerena. Alex collected herself and ran to her room. She scooped the girl up from her crib, stuck her pacifier in her mouth, and rocked her. "Shhhh. I'm sorry I scared you. Mommy's just worried about your *nnenne*. Shhh. It's all right. It's all right." Alex's insides twisted into knots as she tried to comfort her daughter. Carrying the baby in her arms she went to her bedroom to retrieve her cell phone and went back into the living room.

"Hello."

"John, Mama hasn't come home!"

"Okay, calm down."

"Don't tell me to calm down. That restaurant she went to is closed and she isn't home yet."

"Maybe they went somewhere after dinner."

"No." Alex was on the verge of panic. "Something's wrong. I know it."

"Okay. I'm on my way back."

The glare of headlights sweeping into the room drew Alex's attention to the window. "Wait." She exhaled. "I think they just pulled up." She peered through the sheers. "Yes, it's them. I'm sorry I freaked out again."

"You sure you don't want me to come back?"

"Yeah, I'm sure."

"Okay, but take it easy. Breathe."

"Yeah."

"Call me back if you need me."

"I will."

Alex ended the call and stood a few feet from the door with Cerena in her arms and waited. The door opened enough for her to hear her mother on the other side.

"I had a wonderful time tonight, Ade."

"I did as well, Janette. Will I see you tomorrow?"

"Yes, of course."

Alex felt silly listening to the two of them, and quickly dashed to her room with the baby to give them privacy. A few minutes later she heard her mother humming as she made her way up the hall.

Jamilah tapped on Alex's door and poked her head inside the room.

"Well, look who finally made it home," Alex snapped.

"Were you waiting up for me, Mother?"

"Very funny. I tried calling you and you didn't answer. I told you that you don't get charged just for having your cell phone on."

"I know. I'm sorry if I worried you." Jamilah stepped inside carrying her shoes and sat next to Alex on the side of the bed. "But, as you can see there wasn't any reason to be. I'm just fine. Ade is a lovely man. Besides, I knew John was here and I wanted to give you two some time alone. So, after dinner Ade and I drove to Duarte and found this quaint little jazz bar and talked."

"Did you have a nice time?"

"As a matter of fact, I did, despite having to make up most of my past. I almost slipped a couple of times. But, don't worry. As far as Ade Obafemi is concerned, I'm just a harmless old Nigerian widow."

Alex took her mother's hand. "It's been a long time since I've seen you light up like this."

"It's been a very long time since I've enjoyed a man's company so much." Jamilah spied John's wristwatch on Alex's bureau and moved to pick it up. "And I see I wasn't the only one having a good time tonight."

Alex blushed. "Yeah, I guess we got a little carried away. I should feel bad about it but . . ."

"But what?"

"He's still a married man and until he divorces her she still has a claim to him."

"Don't be silly, Omolola. He's not cattle. He has free will. For whatever reason this woman is not the one he wants to be with."

"Yeah, so he keeps telling me."

Jamilah yawned and laid the watch back down. "Well, I guess I better get off to bed. Do you want me to take Cerena?"

"No. I'm gonna keep her in here with me tonight."

"Okay. Good night." Jamilah kissed Alex on the forehead and left the room.

"Good night, Mama."

Alex closed her bedroom door, laid Cerena on the bed, and grabbed John's watch before climbing in next to her. She snapped the band around her wrist and smiled. "No, Chicken Little, the sky is not falling. Get a grip."

9

The next morning Alex was awakened by another bad dream. She looked over to see that Cerena was sucking her thumb and sleeping peacefully, but she couldn't shake the feeling that if something were to happen to her or her mother there would be no one to look after her baby girl. She couldn't fathom her being passed around like a football in the foster care system. Tirrell Ellis was not listed as the father on the birth certificate, but there were other safeguards she felt she could take to ensure Cerena would be taken care of should the unimaginable happen.

She reached for a pad of paper and pen from the drawer of her nightstand.

Tirrell,

I hope you're doing okay. I know I'm the last person you ever thought you'd hear from, but I hope you won't tear this letter up before you read it.

You probably thought I fell off the face of the earth, and under the circumstances couldn't care less one way or the other. Maybe you're hoping I'm dead. The truth is, if you're reading this letter I probably am.

A lot has happened since I last saw you. The biggest thing is that I found out I was pregnant right after I went into protective custody. I know what you must be thinking, but trust me; there was no other man after we hooked up. I had a little girl. Her name is Cerena.

*She was born last August and she's absolutely beauti-
ful. I know every mother says that about their babies,
but she really is. She has your eyes. I can imagine that
this must come as quite a surprise to you. I didn't find
out until a few weeks after I made the deal with the
Attorney General's office and it made me all the more
determined to protect her no matter what.*

*I'm not the monster bitch you think I am. This little
girl is the most important thing in the world to me;
that's why I'm telling you this now. It's time for you to
know the truth. Call it my dying declaration.*

"Shit! What am I doing?" Alex ripped the paper from
the pad and wadded it up. "This is stupid. Why the hell
would I want my daughter to go to that man? The last I
heard he was still in a wheelchair. For all I know he could
still be strung out on crack. I can't do that to my baby. I
won't."

Alex stared at the wad of paper and sat in a quandary,
imagining the worst-case scenario as she glanced over at
Cerena. She was jolted by the ringing of her cell phone
when she reluctantly started on the letter again.

"Hello."

"You're all right?"

"John?"

"I tried to call the house phone and kept getting a busy
signal. I was just about to head over there."

Alex remembered that she'd thrown the phone against
the wall the night before.

"Hey, are you there?"

"Yes, I'm here. I think I must've accidentally knocked
the phone over."

"Is your mother all right?"

"She's fine. I overreacted as usual."

"I told you I'm not going to let anything happen to you."

"I believe you."

"I want to see you later. I think you have something that belongs to me."

Alex smiled and toyed with the band of the watch. "Maybe."

"I think you have my watch, too."

She blushed at his not-too-subtle implication.

"Are you going into the boutique today?"

"Yeah. As a matter of fact I should be up getting ready as we speak. I just didn't sleep very well last night."

"Really, because I slept better than I've slept in a long time."

The memory of his touch caused the corners of her mouth to turn up.

"Apparently I didn't do my job right if you couldn't sleep. I hope you'll give me another opportunity."

"Absolutely."

"Can I come by and take you to lunch?"

"Are we planning to eat this time?"

"Always. You got me hard just thinking about it."

She glowed like a schoolgirl experiencing her first crush. His seductive tone dispelled the doom she'd felt upon waking up. Stroking the fleshy part of her inner thigh her thoughts drifted, recalling the way he felt inside her. *His hot, wet tongue. His thick, hard . . .* Cerena stirred and forced her to put her lust on hold.

"Cerena's waking up. Why don't we pick this up later?"

Alex disconnected the call, flung the comforter back, and arranged the pillows on her bed to keep the baby from rolling off. She headed into the living room and found Jamilah picking up the discarded telephone and examining the indentation in the plastered wall.

"What in the world happened here?"

"I, uh, had a little accident."

"I can see that."

Alex relocated a large potted schefflera to hide the aftermath of her fit. "See! Good as new."

Jamilah threw up her hands. "Okay, I won't ask." She turned to go into the kitchen. "Coffee?"

"Yes, please."

"Can I get you some breakfast?"

"I've got a better idea," Alex responded as she joined Jamilah in the kitchen. "Why don't I cook breakfast for you?"

"Well, I like the sound of that." Jamilah smiled. "I'll go get the baby. I'm sure she's about ready to eat something too."

When Jamilah went to Alex's room she noticed the wads of paper on the floor and the pad on the bed. She leaned over to pick the girl up and the words "Dear Tirrell" jumped out at her. She was further alarmed by what she read next.

She flew into the kitchen with Cerena tucked under her arm, waving the pad of paper in her free hand. "Alexandra, what is this?"

Alex turned around from the stove, shocked by her carelessness.

"You're writing that man a letter," Jamilah shrieked. "Omolola, what are you thinking?"

"I . . . I . . . I was thinking about Cerena."

Jamilah held up the paper and read aloud: "'You probably thought I fell off the face of the earth, and under the circumstances couldn't care less one way or the other. Maybe you're hoping I'm dead. The truth is, if you're reading this letter I probably am.' This is insane. You can't seriously want him of all people to know about this? What if John finds out? Have you thought about that? We could be dismissed from the program and left to our own devices. Is that what you want?"

Alex took the baby from her mother's arms. "I have to have a plan."

"Why, Alexandra? Nothing is going to happen."

"Anything could happen, Mama. If not Rivera I could be hit by a bus or, God forbid, drop dead of a heart attack."

"Don't be ridiculous. You're perfectly healthy."

"Healthy people die all the time."

"I don't like you talking like this."

"I don't like not having a plan, Mama."

"And this is your plan. To tell this man who is responsible for this madness that he fathered your child. You're going to expose yourself to him and then what?"

"If anything happens I want Cerena to be protected."

Jamilah's breathing became erratic. "Why do you insist on dwelling on the probability that something is going to happen?"

"Mama, please calm down."

Jamilah grabbed her chest and slumped down in a chair at the kitchen table as she began to wheeze and cough. Alex dashed to her bedroom to retrieve her inhaler. She could see the flushed expression on her mother's face when she returned and handed it to her. Jamilah furiously shook the device before sticking it in her mouth and squeezing out a couple of puffs of medicine. Alex took her hand and held on until her breathing returned to normal.

"I'm sorry I upset you."

"I don't want you talking about dying, or death, or getting hit by a bus, or anything like that ever again. Do you hear me?"

A pot of oatmeal boiled over on the stove and distracted them just as Alex started to explain why she felt she needed to let Tirrell Ellis know about Cerena. Alex checked to ensure Jamilah was all right before giving her the baby.

"Alexandra, let me help you."

"No, Mama. I got this. You just sit there and relax."

After cleaning up the mess on the stove Alex prepared a couple of fried eggs and toast, as she reconsidered attempting to make Jamilah understand why she needed to follow through with her intentions, for fear of distressing her to the point of convulsion. "I'm going to call the boutique and tell Celeste that I won't be in today."

"You will do no such thing. I don't need you to sit here and watch over me like I'm some invalid. I had a little trouble breathing but I'm all right now. There is no reason for you to stay home."

"Mama, are you sure you're feeling better?"

"Omolola, this isn't the first asthma attack I've had and it probably won't be the last. I'll be fine. You just get ready and go on to work, and promise me that you won't be writing any more letters to that man, and you won't try to contact him in any way."

Alex nodded. Lying seemed necessary.

An accident on the 210 caused Alex to be forty minutes later for work than she thought she might be. After the morning she'd already had, the notion that nothing was going to go right for her today hovered like ominous storm clouds. Her apology was taken in stride as she rushed through the front of the shop teeming with customers, and continued to the back area to secure her purse. She envied the ladies of leisure who had nothing better to do with their time on a Sunday afternoon than to splurge on lavish martini lunches, charity events, and shopping. She fondly recalled the days when she was numbered among them and given the privilege of planning such affairs. Despite her lucrative alliance with drug traffickers, she enjoyed being an event planner, and she was good at it. She thought how mortified she'd be if one of her former clients were to stumble into La Bella and see just how far she'd fallen. She knew all too well if she could be identified as Alexandra Solomon they would all be relocated and the entire process would start over again, new identities and all. Should that happen her biggest regret would be saying good-bye to John Chase.

"Excuse me, Miss. Can you tell me if these shoes come in a size eight?"

Alex looked up from the display she was setting and came face to face with Caren Wallace, the woman she remembered John introducing her to. "I'd be happy to go check in the back for you."

The woman's gaze narrowed. "You look so familiar to me. I know you from somewhere, don't I?"

Alex saw no reason to deny it should the woman call her on it. "We met at the coffee shop in Monrovia on West Foothill a little over a week ago."

"Oh yes. You were with John Chase, weren't you?"

Before she could answer Lorraine Chase stepped up beside her. "Caren, look what I found."

Caren Wallace pursed her thin lips together as the corners of her mouth curled up maliciously. "Look what I found."

Alex's throat constricted and she clenched her teeth.

"Lorraine, this is the woman I was telling you I saw with John at that coffee shop. What was your name again, dear?"

Alex never dealt with being backed into a corner very well. Responding, "Bitch, you don't wanna mess with me," crossed her mind. "Adriane," she answered instead.

"Of course, that's right. Adriane Sullivan, wasn't it?"

"It still is last time I checked," Alex snapped.

Lorraine gave Alex the once-over and snarled, "So, you know my husband?"

Alex remained poised. "It would seem so."

"You waited on me last Thursday when I came to pick up my dresses and never said a word."

"I wasn't aware that I was under any obligation to share any of the details of a chance encounter, Mrs. Chase."

"Well, perhaps it was more than serendipity that brought you two together," Lorraine retorted.

"Are you implying that there's something scandalous going on between me and your husband?"

"Scandalous," Lorraine repeated. "Interesting word choice. Is there something going on that you're just dying to tell me about, Ms. Sullivan?"

Alex stood staring at the woman, wanting to scream, "Yes, there's something going on. I fucked him and it was good. In fact, it was better than good; it was fan-fucking-tastic!"

"I guess it's true what they say," Caren interjected. "It really is a small world."

Lorraine arched her brow, and combed through her fiery mane with her fingers. "And getting smaller every day." She turned her attention back to the garments in her hand. "Caren, what do you think of this one? John always did love me in lace."

"You wear this and I'm sure he wouldn't be able to think about anything else."

Lorraine cut her eyes toward Alex and smiled cattily to her friend. "What do you think, Ms. Sullivan?"

Alex sucked in her cheeks before responding, "I don't really have an opinion."

"Somehow I doubt that," Lorraine asserted.

Caren Wallace chuckled. "Well, I think it's wickedly divine."

"The question is how long would I be wearing it before John ripped it off me? I should probably buy several. The man does have an insatiable appetite."

Alex resisted the urge to add that John also had the stamina of a bull.

"On second thought, it's a little cheap." Lorraine tossed the lingerie on the counter. "Why don't we go someplace where the merchandise isn't quite so . . . scandalous."

Alex rolled her eyes as Lorraine sailed out of the shop with the disingenuous blonde trailing her.

"I wanna play," squealed the freckled tyke, pulling on her father's pant leg.

"Hang on, sweet pea. I'm just about to beat your brother," John replied, looking away from the screen.

"Score! I won!" John Michael yelled, relishing his father's defeat.

John slapped his forehead and fell back on the over-stuffed sofa, feigning disappointment of his Wii tennis skills. He surrendered the game controller to his daughter under his son's protest.

"She's too little to play."

"John Michael, you have to give your sister equal time, otherwise, how is she going to get as good as you and beat her old man?"

The boy frowned.

"C'mon now, you just beat me with one arm in a cast. I tell you what, if you can beat your sister I'll give you five dollars."

Chloe perked up. "Can I have five dollars too, Daddy?"

John tickled her. "I'll give you ten if you beat your brother."

John Michael rose to the challenge and pressed the button on the controller to start another game. John lifted his daughter in his lap and guided her arms and hands into making a volley. The girl jumped up and down cheering as if she'd scored on her own.

"Hey, that's no fair."

John laughed. "I didn't say I was going to make winning easy for you."

Lorraine entered the family room carrying an armload of packages. Chloe forgot all about her game and scurried to see if there was anything for her.

"John Michael, do you really think you should be playing that game?"

"He's all right, Lorraine. He's using his good arm."

She laid her packages down. "John, can I talk to you before you go running off?"

John shot her a side-glance and complied. "John Michael, why don't you take your sister upstairs so your mom and I can talk?"

"But we haven't finished the game," John Michael objected.

John reached into his wallet, extracted five single bills and handed them to his son. "You won."

"What about me?" Chloe pouted.

John fished out another single and gave it to his daughter. "You won too."

The boy pocketed the cash and teased his sister as they went up the stairs about the fact that he had more money than she did.

Lorraine waited until they had cleared the landing. "Have you been here long?"

"We've been home about an hour. After we left the movies we went for pizza."

She grimaced. "Pizza? John, you know I don't like them filling up on junk food. Now, they're not going to want to go to Mom and Dad's later for dinner. I wish you had checked with me first."

"I didn't realize I needed to run my itinerary by you when it came to spending time with my kids."

"That's not what I meant and you know it. Mom and Dad asked about you."

"I can't imagine that."

"Believe it or not, they're not happy about this separation."

"They do know it was your idea, right?"

Lorraine pretended not to hear him.

John pressed on. "Considering how Liam felt about the wedding I would think he'd be dancing an Irish jig that we're not together."

"That's not true. Dad knows how I feel about you, he always has. All he wants is for me to be happy. And you know that Mom wants us back together even if your mother doesn't."

John picked up his jacket from the arm of the sofa and headed toward the living room. Lorraine followed.

"Why don't you come to dinner with us? I know John Michael and Chloe would really love it if you did. We all had such a good time the night of the recital that I thought we could maybe . . ." She pressed into him and tried to kiss him again.

He moved away. "It's not gonna happen again, Lorraine. And I'm not going to sit around the table sharing a meal with your parents while everybody pretends that we're all just one big happy family."

"The way you kissed me. The way you responded to my touch. I know you still have feelings for me."

"I still care about you, Lorraine."

"You just can't admit it to yourself, can you, John?"

"Admit what?"

"That you still love me."

John grabbed his keys from the credenza in the foyer and started to the door.

"Is Adriane waiting for you?"

He halted, but didn't turn back to her. "What?"

"She is the woman you're 'protecting,' isn't she?"

"You know I can't talk about—"

"Yeah, I know. I know. You can't talk about your cases."

"Lorraine—"

"Are you sleeping with her?"

"I gotta go."

"Is she a criminal or a witness? Is she the first one? Have there been others? You've become so adept at the subterfuge . . . this dual identity. Running off in the middle of the night to come to someone else's aid. Is it any wonder why I did what I did? At the end of the day there wasn't any of you left for your family because you gave so much away. I know you have other cases. Why is this one so special?"

John didn't answer.

Lorraine dug in. "Do you know how much trouble you could be in if someone were to find out about what you're doing?"

Thinking about what his stepfather had said to him John spun around and charged back into the room. "You listen to me. I don't know what kind of bull Caren Wallace has filled your head with, but there is absolutely nothing going on for you to worry about, you got that?" The sting of the lie burned on his tongue almost as quickly as it came out of his mouth.

"Don't worry, John. I don't have any intention of soiling your valued reputation or blowing your 'case.' Go ahead. You don't want to keep your girlfriend waiting."

John inhaled deeply and blew his breath out slowly. "You know what, I was going to wait to have this discussion with you. But maybe it's time we start talking about making this separation permanent."

Lorraine scoffed. "You want a divorce."

"Clearly we can't keep going in circles like this." John took a few steps away from her and lowered his head. "You can't be surprised. It's been a long time coming."

Lorraine closed her eyes to keep tears that were form-ing from falling. "When I saw her at the boutique today I wasn't sure if there was really anything between you. But I can see it in your eyes. I hear it in your tone. The way you reacted when I called her your girlfriend. I wish I had told her what we did the other night. I wish I had told her that I wasn't just going to lie down and let her take you from me."

"Take me," John sneered. "I'm not a toy, Lorraine, that you pull out and play with at will. Yeah, I screwed up. I worked too much, too long, but that didn't give you the right to go off and fuck somebody else. You just want me to forget about that, huh? Act like everything is the way it used to be? That is what you want, isn't it?"

Despite Lorraine's resolve, silent, bitter tears streamed down her face. She stood there holding herself together and watched helplessly as John tore out of the house.

John picked Alex up from work and they drove into Los Angeles. Initially she wondered why he was so sullen, but surmised that his disposition had to do with something Lorraine may have said about her. She didn't ask, and he didn't bring it up. Whether he was separated or not what they were doing had all the earmarks of a tawdry affair. She was allowing herself to become exactly what she swore she didn't want to be. She wanted to tell him to take her back to her car, but the words dissipated as quickly as they formed on her lips. He reached over, took her hand, and kissed it. The gesture informed her that his mood was lightening and the consequences be damned.

"Are you sure your mother doesn't mind us spending the night out?"

"She encouraged it. Besides, I think she's preparing a home-cooked meal for Ade."

"Are you still nervous about him being with her?"

"I'm trying to be happy for her. She deserves someone after all she gave up for me."

"And what about you?"

"What do you mean?"

"Don't you deserve someone special too?"

"Do you mean you, Inspector?"

Seconds ticked by in silence until John spoke again. "I lied to Lorraine. She accused me of sleeping with you. A week ago that would've been true, even though I thought about it . . . a lot. I told her that we weren't."

"So, now you feel guilty for lying?"

"I just didn't want her causing any problems."

"For you?"

"For either of us."

"I'm not afraid of her," Alex declared.

John chuckled. "No, I didn't think that you would be."

More silence.

"John, is there something else bothering you?"

"I kissed her." He glanced over to see that Alex was staring straight ahead, emotionless. "We were celebrating my daughter's dance recital and I guess I just got caught up."

"Caught up? What happened to 'I can't stop thinking about you, Alex. You got to me. I want you so bad'?" She cut her eyes toward him and pulled her hand away. "Did you fuck her?"

John exhaled loudly and his jaws tightened.

"Oh, I'm sorry," Alex sneered. "That was so crass and unladylike. Let me put it another way, did you make love to your wife? Hell, I just realized how ridiculous that sounded. I'm asking you if you slept with your own wife."

"Alex—"

"Just forget I asked."

John pressed on. "No. I didn't sleep with her. The kiss . . . it was just an impulse."

"Like being with me?"

"You are not an impulse."

"Then what am I, John? I don't think we ever clearly defined this . . . this . . . whatever it is."

John sighed. "Do you want me to take you home?"

She didn't respond.

He pulled the truck over to the curb and turned off the ignition. "I made a mistake. I'm sorry. There were some feelings . . . some issues. The point is whatever I had with Lorraine is over. I knew that the moment we kissed. You were the one I was thinking about."

"You were kissing her and thinking about me? How charming," Alex cracked. "When you're with me are you thinking about her?"

"What the hell kind of question is that?"

"One that deserves an answer."

"Baby, I only want to be with you. I told you about the kiss because I didn't want it to come between us. I don't know what else to say."

"Say you won't hurt me. If you want Lorraine then go be with her, but don't do this to me." There they were again: all those gushy female emotions of neediness and insecurity that she hated but couldn't insulate herself from. The very reactions that made her recognize that she was no different from any other woman on the planet. "You told me once that you weren't going to beg. I don't beg either, John."

He reached out, caressed her cheek, and pulled her into a long, slow kiss. "You are an exciting, exhilarating, irritating, sexy-ass woman. God help me, I just want you. It's not going to be easy, you know that, right? I need to know if you can deal with this."

Alex considered a bitchy retort, but in her heart she wanted him as much as he professed to want her. She nodded.

John started up the truck and continued up the street.

They were greeted by a balmy Southern California breeze when they stepped out of the truck on Melrose, where he escorted her into the Larchmont Grill. John seemed a lot more relaxed now. His cavalier attitude was amusing and exhibited a bit more of a rakish side than she'd seen prior to the consummation of their relationship. She fussed with her hair and smoothed down her skirt as they were seated.

"You look beautiful." He smiled.

"I can't help thinking that we might run into more of your and Lorraine's friends."

"So, what if we do? You said you could handle it, right?"

"You like living dangerously," she mused.

"I gotta admit, it does turn me on." He chuckled. "But, not nearly as much as you do."

Dinner went off without as much as an unsolicited glance from a stranger. They sat like unabashed lovers feeding one another from their dishes and laughing as if they didn't have a care between them.

"Was your food all right? You didn't eat much," John noted.

Alex licked her lips. "I'm planning on having a big dessert."

He chuckled. "Is that right?"

"A nice long cream-filled chocolate éclair."

"I don't think they have that on the menu."

Alex ran her hand under the table and up his leg. "Then I guess we'll have to find some place that can satisfy my craving."

John inhaled sharply and his nostrils flared. "So, do you think it would be all right if I were to get us a hotel room when we leave here?"

"I'm willing if you are."

***

John dropped his sports jacket as they stepped onto the elevator of the Marriott and fumbled with the buttons of Alex's blouse like he was enthusiastically unwrapping an anticipated gift. She pulled and undid his belt with aplomb and dropped to her knees, unleashing his penis and taking its girth into her mouth. He leaned back against the wall and moaned. They jumped when the elevator dinged. Without enough time to pull himself together, John grabbed his jacket to cover himself. Alex unsuccessfully stuffed the tail of her blouse back into the waistband of her skirt, leaving her lace black bra exposed.

An older woman stepped in and sneered, "Humph," shooting them a side-glance of disdain. John cleared his throat and snorted. Alex buried her face into his chest to stifle her laughter. They exited the elevator, falling into one another, and left the elderly woman rolling her eyes and grunting with displeasure.

"You are something else," John observed, taking the keycard and opening the door to the room.

"You ain't seen nothin' yet, Inspector," Alex replied.

Once inside the room they yanked the covers back from the bed, disrobed, and licked, sucked, and thrust their way into carnal euphoria.

"Damn, I needed that," Alex purred like a satisfied kitten. "After the way this day started I thought it was going to be a complete bust, but being with you here . . . now . . . makes it all worth it."

"I'm glad I could help." John pulled her into a kiss. "You're pretty wild, you know that?"

"Are you complaining?"

"Not at all. I'm just glad I could keep up."

Alex swept the hair from her face and sat up on her elbows. She caressed the hairs of his leg with her foot and played with his flaccid penis. "Care to 'keep up' one more time?"

John pretended to be asleep and snored.

"Uh-huh, I know you are not asleep."

He laughed and opened his eyes, and pulled her over on top of him. "You keep this up and you're never going to get rid of me."

"Well, maybe I don't want to get rid of you," she responded.

"That's a good thing."

"Oh, yeah?"

"Absolutely."

He rolled her over, nibbling her earlobes and neck. His hands pinned hers to the bed and she squirmed as his tongue licked the salty residue of sex from her skin. She inhaled deeply and held her breath as his lips worked her prone nipples in concert. When he released her hands she cradled his shaven head close to her bosom and kissed it. His fingertips glided down her stomach as if plucking out a tune on a keyboard, making their way back to her clitoris. She opened her legs, allowing him full access as he stimulated her into another quivering climax. When she was fully satisfied he lay on his side and pulled her into him, entwining the strength of his legs into the firm softness of hers as they drifted off to sleep.

After dancing around the forbidden for months, they were finally together. And in that moment nothing and no one else mattered.

10

Federal and state insignias, service accommodations, plaques, and stoic portraits of bureaucrats lined the walls leading into the marshal's office. Acrylic diffusers covered fluorescent ceiling lights emitting white noise and muting their everyday office routine. Harley Donovan leaned back in his chair with his boots propped up on his oak wood desk, perusing the contents of a confidential document and whistling "The Yellow Rose of Texas."

"You're late," he barked, as John rushed in. Impishly peering over the documents he resembled a praying mantis with the deep warm green of his gaze. "Where ya been, buddy?"

John pulled off his jacket and threw it over his chair. "I overslept."

"Bullshit. You haven't overslept since you stopped suckin' your mama's tit."

John poured his coffee and shot a look over his shoulder. "To hell with you, Harley."

"You were with a woman, weren't you? You and Lorraine gettin' back together?"

"Mind your business, Donovan," John snapped. He sat down to his desk and logged in to his computer.

"Somethin's different about you." The man stood up and sniffed around John's chair like a bloodhound. "You had sex last night."

John recoiled. "Hey, back the hell up, man."

Donovan combed his fingers through his thick, wavy dark brown hair and folded his arms. "Well, I'll be damned." He leaned on John's desk and whispered, "You did it, didn't you?"

"Did what?"

"You finally banged that Sullivan chick?"

John pushed back from his desk and stood up. "This coffee's disgusting."

"Don't try to deny it. It's written all over your face, and probably your cock, too."

"My cock," John jeered, pouring more sugar into his cup. "You sound like some overrated porn star."

The man laughed. "What word would you prefer I use that wouldn't offend your delicate sensibilities, dick, johnson, schlong, man meat? Either way you hit that, didn't you?"

John set his coffee cup down, grabbed Donovan by the arm, and pulled him aside. "Will you keep your voice down?"

"Don't get me wrong, man. I'm all for satisfying the libido. If you're gettin' a little action on the side that's your prerogative."

"Harley, come on, man."

"What? That woman is fine as frog's hair. If she even looked at me twice I'd be all over that."

John shoved his hands into his pockets and sighed. "Are you gonna give me shit about this?"

"Do I need to?"

"It just happened, that's all. We didn't plan it."

"No, sir. That did not just happen." Donovan laughed.

"Dude, will you shut the hell up?"

Noting John's growing irritation Donovan lowered his voice. "That particular cat's been scratchin' at that post for a long time. I knew you'd cave sooner or later. Every time she calls you go runnin', anytime, night or day. I can't say that I blame you though."

"Look, you can't . . . You're not gonna tell Toliver about this, are you?"

Donovan glanced around to see who among the three other people in the office might be listening. "How long have we been partners?"

John shrugged his shoulder. "Hell, I don't know. Four years."

"Five." Donovan corrected him. "I got this assignment January 16, 2005. I remember 'cause it was the day after I lost Bear. Havin' to put my dog down was somethin' I'll never forget. Somethin' like that stays with you, you know what I mean?"

"So, what's your point, Harley?"

"My point is we've been through some rough times together. We went through them as partners. Hey, I'm Uncle Donny, right? I got your back, my friend."

"Yeah, well, I hope so."

"What? Are you doubtin' me now? You know you can trust me, John. Besides, if I was an enemy you'd know it."

"Oh, really?"

"Yeah, it's like my granddaddy Herman always said, 'your best enemies are the ones you don't see comin'.' Just don't let this thing you're doin' make you lose focus."

John went back to his coffee cup. "Now this shit is cold."

Donovan pressed on. "So, what are you gonna do?"

"About what?"

"C'mon, you know what I'm talkin' about."

"I don't know yet."

"Well, while you're decidin' do you mind if I give Lorraine a call?"

John looked at the man as if he should already know what his response would be.

Donovan threw up his hands. "Hey, I was just checkin'. At any rate you need to figure out what you're gonna do

about this Sullivan situation before it goes south on you.
You've heard the expression you don't shit where you eat.
You wouldn't be the first hombre who let his dick get him
into trouble. And gettin' that particular cat back in the
bag is gonna be a helluva lot harder than when you let it
out."

"Let me guess, another wise old saying from your dear
ol' Granddaddy Herman."

Donovan laughed. "Man, I could write a book."

"I think that subject has already been covered." John
chuckled. "It's called *You Might Be a Redneck If*. You
know you look a lot like the dude who wrote it."

Donovan smirked. "Ha! Ha!"

The bell on the door drew Alex's attention from the
customer she was checking out at the counter. The sight
of Lorraine Chase unnerved her. Momentarily distracted
she ran the credit card in her hand upside down through
the terminal. She quickly righted herself, bagged the
woman's purchases, and completed the transaction.

One of the other clerks made her way over to Lorraine
to see if she could be of assistance.

"No, thank you," Lorraine responded and continued to
the register.

Alex mounted her game face. "Is there something I can
do for you, Mrs. Chase?"

"Do you know why I'm here, Ms. Sullivan?"

"I assume you either have an exchange, or there's something else you're interested in purchasing."

"I wouldn't be so glib if I were you. We need to talk
and I don't think you want me to make a scene in front of
these people, do you?"

Alex cut her eyes toward Margot, who was dressing
a mannequin near the window and gazing at them with
gossip-mongering interest.

Undaunted, Lorraine stood and eyed Alex as if to intimidate her. Alex glared back defiantly.

"We can either have this conversation here, or we can go somewhere else, Ms. Sullivan. Either way I'm not leaving here before I say what I came to say."

Alex sucked in her cheeks. "All right. I'll meet you outside in the square."

Celeste approached them. "Mrs. Chase, is there a problem?"

"No, not at all," Lorraine said without taking her gaze away from Alex. "I just need to have a few words with Ms. Sullivan. We need to clear up a personal matter." With that Lorraine turned and left the shop in a fragrant whoosh of Giorgio.

"Celeste, I need to take a quick break. This shouldn't take long," Alex said evenly. Not waiting for the woman to respond, Alex cinched the leather sash of her dress and followed Lorraine into the quadrant surrounding the boutique. She didn't want a fight but if there were to be a physical altercation, given her Bronx, New York upbringing, she was confident that Lorraine Chase was ill matched.

Lorraine began by lobbing an insult. "I find it curious how you can afford to wear Armani. You can't be making that much working here."

"You don't know what I can afford. And I seriously doubt if you're here to critique my wardrobe," Alex shot back.

"Fine, I'll get to the point, Adriane, or whatever your name is."

The caustic snipe "whatever your name is" gave Alex pause. She didn't know exactly what, if anything, Lorraine knew about her. She didn't want to make any assumptions. Alex peered over her shoulder back toward the shop window to see Margot and another salesgirl peering out. She shifted her position behind a terracotta fountain angling out from the side of the building to force Lorraine out of their sightline.

"What do you want, Mrs. Chase?"

Lorraine pulled her sunglasses from the crown of her stylish bob and slid them up the bridge of her nose. "I don't know what my husband has told you about our relationship, but I can assure you that he's not going to do anything that would put you over the welfare of his children."

Alex's gaze narrowed. "Excuse me."

Lorraine inched closer. "Don't feign innocence, Ms. Sullivan. It doesn't suit you. Please don't insult me by pretending nothing is going on between the two of you."

"I'm not going to insult you by pretending anything, Mrs. Chase. And I won't give you the benefit of defending myself against your groundless speculations. The only reason I came out here to speak to you is to keep my business *my* business. If there are problems in your marriage you may want to take a long, hard look in the mirror. "

"I don't know what delusions you've conjured up about you and my husband being together, but it's never going to happen."

"You know what, I don't have the time or the energy for this discussion." Alex sidestepped Lorraine and started back. "If you're going to fight for John, you should be sure it's a fight you can win."

"Did he tell you what happened between us the night we went to our daughter's dance recital? He came back to the house after . . . Our house."

Alex huffed. "And the two of you kissed. Yes, he told me."

"Oh, it was a lot more than that. I suspect he didn't tell you everything."

In that moment Alex thought about all the other women like Lorraine she'd encountered in her lifetime, and she knew just how to put an end to this tiresome presumption. "Let me ask you something, Lorraine, where was all this determination to hold on to your husband when you cheated on him? If the time you spent together was so all-consuming why are you even here? Why the hell do you feel threatened by me? Is all of this desperation worth holding on to someone who doesn't want to be held on to?"

Lorraine's pinched expression said everything that needed to be said.

"That's what I thought," Alex sneered. "Have a good day, Mrs. Chase." With that she sashayed back inside the boutique.

"What was that about?" Margot asked.

"It was nothing," Alex replied. "Just a misunderstanding."

Alex disregarded the glances exchanged between Margot, the salesgirl, and two other customers.

By that afternoon the backlash from Lorraine's visit came back to bite her in the ass. Lorraine had rallied her resources and friends and threatened to boycott La Bella if Alex wasn't "dealt with."

Celeste poked her head out of her office door. "Adriane, can I talk to you?"

Alex smirked, shook her head, and went into the woman's office, expecting the worst. She would not be disappointed.

Celeste was seated behind her marble-top desk with a sober expression on her face and her weathered hands clasped in front of her. "Close the door and have a seat," Celeste instructed.

Alex complied.

"I just got off the phone with Lorraine Chase. I'm not happy with what she had to tell me concerning her visit with you earlier today. I've also been on the phone with several of our regular patrons . . . all of them complaining about you. I—"

"You're firing me," Alex interrupted.

"I hope you understand that we can't have you working here under these circumstances. It would be very bad for business. I'm sorry, Adriane. Your last check will be sent to you by mail."

"Fine. I'll get my things."

Alex's unceremonious departure wasn't completely unforeseen. Driving home she pulled the $300 Italian silk scarf she'd taken as a parting gift from her purse and smirked. The gauntlet had been thrown down. She couldn't know what else Lorraine Chase had up her sleeve. But, she knew better than anyone that a scorned woman was a dangerous woman. This was a setback, but it wouldn't be the last.

Her cell phone rang. It was John.

"Hello."

"Hey, how're you doing?"

"I'm fine."

"You sound funny. Is something wrong?"

"I had an interesting encounter with your wife again today."

"What did she say?"

"She implied that something more was going on with the two of you than what you told me."

John scoffed. "I thought she might."

"She said you weren't going to do anything to hurt your children, and I assume that means that she has no intention of giving you up without a fight."

"There's nothing left for her to fight for," John responded.

"She doesn't seem to agree with that assessment. And I guess it didn't help that I baited her," Alex countered.

"It doesn't matter," John assured her. "Listen, I really want to spend some time with you. Do you want to grab some dinner after you get off work tonight?"

"Well, thanks to your lovely wife I no longer have a job."

"What did she do?"

"Apparently several complaints came in shortly after she left. Celeste didn't want to lose her most valuable customers, so I became expendable."

"Dammit," John spat.

"Don't worry about it. She did exactly what I would have done if I was in her shoes. It's just a job. I found that one, I can get another one."

"What are you doing now?"

"I'm on my way home."

"I'm going to go and have a little talk with Lorraine. Can I call you later?"

"John, please don't do anything that's going to make things worse."

"Don't worry. I'll handle Lorraine."

Anticipating a visit from her estranged husband, Lorraine sent the children to her parents. She was seated at the bar, working on her third martini, when John charged into the foyer.

"Lorraine!"

She closed her eyes and braced herself but didn't respond.

"What the hell is going on?"

She spun around to face him. "I'm having a drink. Would you care for one?"

"No, I don't want a drink. Tell me why you went to that boutique this afternoon and why you confronted Adriane Sullivan?"

"I had to get your attention somehow."

John's jaw clenched and his nostrils flared. Lorraine stood and steadied herself before she walked over to him. She caressed his face and neck. He grabbed her hand and shoved her away. "You did this to get my attention? You had an affair to get my attention? Well, you got it, now what?"

"Now we put everything behind us and remember the things that brought us together in the first place. I want us to work, John. I'd do anything to make that happen."

He shook his head and paced the room. "You're something else, you know that? This is bullshit."

"If it weren't for that woman we'd be on our way back to each other right now."

"You're deluding yourself, Lorraine."

"I know what it meant when you kissed me. When you held me. When we—"

"Did you tell her that we slept together?"

"No, I didn't tell her that."

"But you implied it?"

"You're still my husband."

"Did you get her fired, too?"

"I simply told the owner of the boutique that I was taking my business elsewhere. If she fired the bitch it's not my fault."

"You know damn well she's not the reason we're separated."

Lorraine's eyes filled with tears. "How long are you going to punish me for that?"

"Is that what you think I'm doing?"

"You weren't there for us, John. You were hardly ever there. You made me feel like I didn't matter . . . like we didn't matter. Do you know how hard it was to watch you run off in the middle of the night on one case after another? Every time I heard a siren my heart would stop. Every time the phone rang and you weren't lying next to me I thought I was going to be told that something had happened to you."

"I can forgive what you did. I can even understand it, but I can't forget it."

"Because of her, right? Don't stand there and lie to my face, John. At least give me the courtesy of being man enough to tell the truth. Do you even know what that is anymore?"

"Dammit, Lorraine! Why in the hell are you trying so hard to hold on to something that you say caused you so much pain? Why can't you just admit what this is really about, huh? This isn't about how much you love me, or how much you need me. This is about winning and losing. Liam Reardon didn't raise his princess to lose out on anything to anybody. Well, this isn't some fucking beauty pageant!"

"I know this isn't a contest."

"Then let's end this sham of a marriage so we can move on." John sat down and buried his face in his hands.

"So you can move on . . . isn't that what you mean?" Lorraine wiped tears from her eyes and hesitantly moved to the sofa and sat next to him. "We've both made mistakes, but in spite of everything I don't want to let you go. If your family means as much to you as you say, there has to be a part of you that doesn't want to let that go either. I know your work is important to you, but is it more important than being an example to our children? You're only thirty-seven years old, John, and I believe you're still idealistic enough to go back to school. That was your dream. You can have that now."

"Dreams change. People change."

"What is it you're afraid of?"

"I'm not afraid of anything." John pushed up off the sofa, went to the bar, and poured himself a shot of bourbon.

"The first time we met you were working security at one of my mother's parties and I made a joke about you being one of the best-looking rent-a-cops I'd seen. I flirted with you the entire night."

"We've already been down memory lane more times than necessary."

Lorraine stood up and faced him as he poured another shot. "You were working your way through law school. I fell in love with you because I believed in you. I believed in your dreams. I believed that you wanted to make something more out of your life."

"I did make something out of my life," John angrily fired back. "When I was a cop I was the best damn cop I could be. Now I'm damn proud of being a marshal. If you're so disillusioned then why can't you stop this?"

"Because I know how much I loved you then, how much I still love you."

"Then you should also recall why I gave up that dream. You got pregnant. We got married—"

"And you've blamed me for it in one way or another ever since."

"I stepped up and I took care of my responsibilities the best way I knew how."

"You promised you'd go back to school. Daddy would be happy to—"

"I'm not taking another dime of Liam's money. God knows he would never let me live it down. He already holds this house over my head every chance he gets."

"You paid him back."

"That's not the point. It took every bit of what I saved and a chunk of my self-respect right along with it. But, this is my family and I decide how I choose to take care of them. Next to my kids, this job is the most important thing in the world to me." John tossed back another shot, slammed the glass down on the counter, and walked toward the door. "We can have an amicable divorce. I may not be rollin' in it, but I told you before I would make sure you and the kids had everything you needed. There's no point prolonging the inevitable."

"You weren't so damn eager to run off and get a divorce before Adriane Sullivan came along."

"Lorraine, I want to be able to look at you again and not see you in bed with another man, but I can't. I know that my job has been hard for you to deal with and you'd rather see me in a suit working a nine to five, but that's not who I am."

"I know who you are, John."

"Do you? Or do you just see who you want me to be?"

"What is so wrong with that?"

"Nothing is wrong with that. But, there's absolutely nothing wrong with me. I like who I am, Lorraine. You can blame my job, you can blame Adriane Sullivan, hell, you can blame global warming, but we're not the same people we were before the kids . . . before the house. I didn't destroy what we had all by myself; we both had a hand in it. I'm not doin' this anymore. I'm done." John tossed back another shot and grimaced. "I never pegged you for a martyr. Sometimes when something is broken it should just stay that way."

11

"Happy Birthday, Mama."

Jamilah's eyes lit up when she opened the decoratively colored foil paper. "Omolola, it's beautiful. It's so soft." She rubbed the cashmere material of the sweater against her face.

"There's a skirt that comes with it, too." Alex didn't have the heart to give her mother the stolen scarf, opting instead to keep it for herself and buy her mother something else.

"You shouldn't have done this, Omolola. You can't afford this now that you're not working."

"Of course I can. We're not going to be in the poor house anytime soon. I have money in savings."

"It's called savings for a reason. It's not that I don't appreciate it, but you don't need to spend your money on expensive things."

"If I can't spend my money to buy you something nice on your special day I wouldn't be much of a daughter, would I?"

Jamilah hugged her. "This will be perfect for tonight."

"Tonight?"

"Ade asked if he could take me out to dinner."

"Oh."

Jamilah laid the sweater and skirt aside. "I'm sorry. You didn't have plans, did you?"

"Well, I just thought I'd take you to dinner."

"Oh, Omolola. I could call Ade. I'm sure he'll understand."

Alex took her mother's hands. "You don't have to change your plans on my account. This is your day. You should spend it however you want. We can go to dinner another time. So, you and Ade, huh?"

"Don't say it like that, Alexandra."

"Like what?"

"Like we're fooling around behind the high school bleachers." Jamilah stood and moved to the mirror mounted on her bureau and fussed with her hair. "We're mature adults who enjoy each other's company."

"Mama, I'm glad you found someone you could spend time with other than those biddies you play cards with."

"They're not biddies." Jamilah laughed. "Well, maybe Ernie Mae is." She picked up the sweater and skirt, held it up against her body, and preened in front of the mirror. "Not bad for fifty-eight, eh?"

Alex stood up behind her mother and pulled her hair up away from her neck. "When I'm your age I can only hope to look half as amazing. Now, why don't we see if Miss Ernie Mae can look after Cerena while I treat you to a manicure and pedicure?"

"Omolola, you've done enough. You really don't need to do anything else for me."

"I know I don't have to do it, Mama. I want to. Now don't argue with me. It's your birthday."

In spite of the fact that Jamilah put up a fuss after luxuriating at the day spa, Alex managed to get her stylist to squeeze her in for a hair appointment. Several hours later Jamilah was primped and ready for a night on the town.

The doorbell rang.

"I'll get it." With a quick glimpse out the window Alex verified that it was Ade. She greeted him and invited him inside. "Mama is just finishing up. She should be out shortly."

"It is all right," Ade responded. "I do not mind waiting."

"Would you like to sit down?"

He unbuttoned his suit jacket and sat. "Hello, little one," he directed to Cerena, who was sitting up in her playpen, chewing on a teething ring.

Alex noted how graceful, even gentle, he seemed for a man of his stature. "My mother tells me that you're from Nigeria?"

"Kandula. Very close to Abuja. My family came to the United States some years ago."

"You recently lost your wife?"

"Yes, October, 2008."

"I'm sorry to hear that."

"Janette . . . your mother . . . has been a very pleasant companion. She is a charming woman."

Jamilah made a show of her entrance. "My ears are burning. Is someone talking about me?"

Ade stood and nodded. "You are familiar with the Nigerian word meaning beautiful. It is *jamilah*."

Alex looked at the surprise in her mother's eyes and interrupted. "Uh, before you go, let me get a picture." She dashed to her bedroom for a camera and came back as Ade was hustling Jamilah to the door.

"Wait. Can I get a picture first?"

Jamilah adjusted her wrap and stuck her arm into Ade's, pulling him back into the room. Ade appeared apprehensive. "I usually do not like taking pictures."

"Please," Alex encouraged him.

"You're a handsome man, Ade. Just this one. For me," Jamilah implored.

Jamilah beamed and Ade smiled nervously. He turned his head slightly and looked off when the camera clicked. Alex instantly showed them the scan from her digital camera. "See, that wasn't so bad."

"Oh, Ade. You look like you've lost your best friend. It's just a harmless photograph. Come now, Omolola. Take another one."

"No," Ade said firmly. "We should be going if we are to avoid the traffic."

Alex shot Jamilah a look, but didn't question Ade's resistance. She saw them to the door and waved good-bye.

Once Jamilah and Ade were gone she laid the camera down on the coffee table, reached into the playpen, and picked Cerena up. "All right, my girl. Now that *Nnenne* is out for the evening what do you want to do? Do you wanna go outside for a while?"

Cerena's indecipherable gurgles were taken as a yes. Alex grabbed a small cup of Cheerios from the cupboard and stepped out of the kitchen door that led out to an open patio. She sat with Cerena in her arms and fed her the snack. From her vantage point she could see the crest of the mountains to the west and the crimson glow of the sun balancing over the horizon like a giant air balloon.

"Do you think your father is looking at this very same sun right now?"

Her thoughts were interrupted and she was startled by the crunch of leaves and grass at the side of the house. She bounded from her lounge chair. "Who's there?" She listened to the stillness and crept closer to the door. "Is anyone there?"

Just as she was about to dart back inside two squirrels scampered across the yard and up the side of a tree. She heaved a sigh of relief and decided to go back inside anyway.

After getting Cerena cleaned, changed, and settled, Alex went to the kitchen to find something to eat. She opened the refrigerator and pulled out some cold cuts, mayonnaise, mustard, and pickles, and tried to carry them to the counter all at once.

"Damn," she spat as the jar of mayonnaise slipped from her hand and splattered across the tiled floor.

Hoping the noise hadn't disturbed Cerena, she put the other items down, stepped around the broken glass, and grabbed a towel. Her nerves were rattled further when the doorbell rang. Abandoning the mess she crept close to the door. She wasn't close enough to see out the window or the peephole, so she just stood in the arch between the kitchen and dining room waiting for whoever it was to go away. A knock followed. Practically every light was on in the house and her car was in the driveway. She couldn't have pretended she wasn't home if she wanted to. Glancing around the room her eyes locked on the alarm panel being disarmed, and a lump formed in her throat.

"Adriane?"

She threw her head back and exhaled at the recognition of John's voice. Not giving thought to her appearance, she hurried to open the door.

"What have I told you about opening this door without verifying who it is?"

"You scared the shit out of me," Alex countered nervously.

"I'm sorry. I was just driving through the neighborhood and I saw the lights on. I needed to see you."

She flung herself into his arms and held on. "I'm so glad it's you."

"What's wrong?"

"I've just been feeling a little jumpy tonight, that's all." She released her hold and he stepped into the house after her. She secured the locks and set the alarm.

"Are you here by yourself?"

"No. Cerena's asleep. Weren't you supposed to be with your kids?"

"I was. I just dropped them off. I really didn't expect to find you home. I thought you said you were taking your mother out to dinner."

"That was the plan. We spent the afternoon together, but she ditched me for Ade."

"They're getting pretty serious."

"Seems to be."

"What is that smell?" John said, sniffing the air. "Is that mayonnaise?"

Alex wiped her hands on the legs of her jeans and brushed the hairs of a loosely tied ponytail back behind her ears. "I was making a sandwich and broke a jar on the kitchen floor. I must've gotten some on me. I need to get cleaned up.

"Go ahead." He smiled. "I'll be here when you get back."

John found a mop and bucket. While Alex went to clean up, he finished what she'd started. Twenty minutes later she came back into the living room, looking and smelling a sight better than she had been. She found John engrossed in the last quarter of a Lakers game. Neither his eyes nor his mind lingered on the game. He took her hand, pulled her into his lap, and they kissed.

"Hmmmm," he sighed. "I've been thinking about doing that all day."

"So have I," she purred and inhaled the piney scent emanating from the kitchen. "You mopped?"

"All-purpose inspector at your service."

"Oooh, I like a man who knows how to clean a house."

He kissed her. "I know how to do a lot of things."

"Yes, indeed you do." She chuckled.

"I assume you still haven't eaten?"

"I had a salad for lunch."

"Well, what do you say we order a pizza?"

"That sounds great."

Alex located a delivery in the neighborhood and ordered. She then fixed herself a drink.

"Would you like one?"

"I'll take a beer if you have it."

"I think there's a few Corona in the refrigerator."

"Sounds good. So, how's the job search?"

She passed him a bottle of Corona and sat down next to him on the sofa. "I've got an interview at an art gallery in Glendale on Monday."

"I didn't know you knew that much about art."

"If I can sell clothes I ought to be able to move a few paintings."

"I have no doubt you can do anything you put your mind to."

Alex threw her head back in disgust. "Yeah, that's what got me into shit in the first place. I guess this is just karma biting me in the ass."

John leaned in and kissed her again. "But it's such a cute ass."

Alex smiled and playfully pushed him away.

John took a swig from the bottle and sat with his elbows resting on his thighs. "Do you miss it?"

"Miss what?"

"That world you lived in."

"I miss the feeling of being in charge of my life," Alex replied. "I miss the parties. The clothes. The celebrities. I was good at what I did."

John sat back. "Selling drugs. Do you miss that, too?"

Alex shook her head. "I'm not gonna lie. The perks were pretty damn good. And sometimes it was as exciting for me as all of this is for you. In the beginning after Ray died I was scared out of my mind. I was a nobody. Then I met Xavier Rivera and all kinds of doors started opening up for me. I had my own business. I was traveling and I had money . . . I let my guard down when I got involved with Tirrell Ellis, but at least one good thing came out of all that mess. I have my beautiful baby girl." Alex sighed. "Now, I've screwed up your life."

John stared into Alex's eyes and pulled her into a kiss. "You haven't screwed up anything."

"Liar. You never told me what happened when you went to see Lorraine the other day."

"Other than the fact that I told her to back the hell off there wasn't a whole lot to it. She was singing the same old song about us getting back together, and me going back to law school."

"Something safe?"

"Settling in and being a lawyer was cool before we had kids and the big house that I couldn't afford. But, I did what I had to do to support my family. I don't have any regrets about that." John turned up the bottle and sucked down the Corona.

"Can I get you another one?"

"How about something a little stronger?"

By the time the pizza arrived and two drinks later, John had mellowed. He was even laughing about how much of a disappointment he'd been to Lorraine's father and her Irish Catholic upbringing.

"So, if her father thought you were beneath her why did he let the two of you get married?" Alex queried.

"Because Lorraine told him she was pregnant and he didn't want her to bring shame on the precious Reardon name."

"Was she?"

"No. John Michael was born a year after we got married. Liam, her father, thought I put Lorraine up to the lie so I could get me hands on her Lucky Charms."

Alex laughed at John's bad attempt to affect an Irish brogue. He was so charismatic. It was easy to see how Lorraine or any woman could fall so completely for him and lament losing him. And there it was again: that heartrending look in his soulful brown eyes. In that moment she intuitively knew of at least one unspoken regret. Locked away inside of him was the tarnished love he once had for Lorraine, and possibly still did regardless of what he said.

Ade's cell phone rang as he and Jamilah were finishing dinner. He blanched when he looked at the caller ID.

"Ade, is something wrong?"

"No," he responded. "It's just my daughter. "Will you excuse me for a moment?"

She smiled politely. He got up from the table and went toward the men's room for privacy.

"What is it?"

"*¡Hola! mi amigo.*"

The mocking tone of the caller resonated in Ade's ear. He closed his hand over his mouth.

"I trust you are enjoying your evening out with the lovely *señora*."

Ade backed into the wall to allow a man coming from the men's room to pass.

"*Señor* Obafemi, are you there?"

"Y . . . yes. I'm here."

"It's time to move our plan forward."

"I . . . I can't."

"You can and you will, or else—"

"There has to be another way."

"Don't tell me you are getting cold feet."

"I don't want to hurt these people."

"Would you rather your family be hurt instead?"

"No."

"Then you know what has to be done, yes?"

Ade nodded as if his silent compliance could be heard. He ended the call and hesitantly returned to the table.

"Is everything all right?"

"Everything is fine. I should get you home."

Ade tried not to show that he was troubled on the ride back. He knew what was coming and feared the reprisal against his children if he didn't go through with it. Like the gentleman he'd presented he saw Jamilah to the door. The porch light was on and only Alex's Honda Civic was parked in the driveway.

Jamilah smiled. "Thank you for making my birthday something special."

"It was my pleasure."

She reached out and caressed his face.

"'O Thou bright jewel in my aim I strive to comprehend thee.'"

Ade's eyes clouded. He leaned in and kissed her good night: a Judas kiss tinged with betrayal.

12

"Ah, look a' here. That's what I'm talkin' about. Keep 'em comin', Pauline." The whiskey-voiced Ernie Mae laughed and taunted as the cards were dealt. "Come on, Janette. We're about to sweep the floor with these two."

"How many books do we need?" Jamilah asked, sitting down to the table with a pitcher of lemonade.

"Five."

"If we run a Boston you all won't get one book, let alone five," Pauline, the dealer, snapped as she picked up her cards.

"Just don't renege again, like you did last time," Ernie Mae retorted.

The woman sitting to the right of Jamilah peered over her bifocals and smirked as she set her hand in order. "So, Janette, how was your date last night?"

"It was really nice, Margaret. Ade took me to Lagos."

The women looked confused.

"It's the place in Los Angeles that serves African cuisine. It used to be called Ngoma," Jamilah clarified. "The evening was an absolute delight and Ade was the perfect gentleman."

"Gentleman, huh?" Ernie Mae smirked. "You give him any yet?"

"Shhhh," Pauline chided. She craned her neck toward the living room where Cerena watched them from her playpen.

"What?" Ernie Mae laughed. "That baby don't know what we're talkin' about. Besides, ain't none of us gettin' any younger. We got to get it whenever and wherever we can. Truth be told, if I had my say, I'd take a glass of that tall, dark drink of water I see cattin' around over here a couple of nights a week. Girl, that man is fine. Young and hard beats old and saggy any day."

"Ernie Mae, you so bad. Janette, I don't know how you put up with her." Pauline covered her mouth to stifle her amusement.

"Hey, just keepin' it real, like my grandson says."

Jamilah grimaced. "Are we goin' to play cards, or are we goin' to cackle like a bunch of old hens?"

The three women—resembling some sort of barnyard fowl or the other—exchanged telling glances and then eyed Jamilah. Ernie Mae was the only one brazen enough to continue prying.

"Girl, what happened? Is he bad in bed? Oh, I get it. He's not regulation size, is he?"

Jamilah pursed her lips together and frowned.

Pauline leaned in to whisper, "He doesn't need that Viagra stuff, does he?"

Cerena's jubilant laughter drew the women's attention and they all laughed as well.

Margaret peered over her bifocals again. "Maybe she does know what we're talking about."

"That ain't nothin' but gas," Ernie Mae quipped.

"Can we just play cards, please?" Jamilah injected. "Corruptin' my grandchild with this nonsense . . . I got four uptown."

The bidding continued around the table until all the women were in. As the game progressed, Ernie Mae persisted in goading Jamilah regarding Ade's prowess, or lack thereof.

"Well, the important thing is I have a man who's interested in me, which is more than I can say for you," Jamilah retorted. "And trust me, when the time is right it's goin' to be everything I need it to be and more."

"All righty then," Pauline snapped giving Jamilah a high five.

"I guess she told you," Margaret added.

"Y'all losers can pay up and kiss my fat, yellow ass," Ernie Mae sneered, slapping down the winning card.

"Uh-oh," Jamilah said, getting up from the table. "Somebody needs changin'."

The women got a whiff of the air in the room and unanimously agreed that it was a good time to bring their afternoon to a close.

Ernie Mae snagged a handful of cheese and crackers on her way out the door. "Don't forget to cash those social security checks, ladies. Next week's game is at my house."

The other two women said their good-byes and followed her out. After they left, Jamilah hoisted Cerena from the playpen and hustled her to the bathroom to clean her up. Once she was done with that she went back to the kitchen for a bottle. She noticed Margaret's bifocals on the table and picked them up as the doorbell rang.

"I figured you'd be back," she said, opening the door.

She was greeted by the sight of a balding man with old burn scars on the left side of his face. He was dressed in a plain dark suit, holding what appeared to be religious tracts.

"Excuse me, ma'am. I was wondering if I might have a few minutes of your time to talk about Judgment Day."

Jamilah looked past him into the driveway and spied a black van. It wasn't the same as Alex described to the police a few weeks earlier, but instinctively she felt something wasn't right. She attempted to slam the door in his face, but he pushed up against it with his shoulder and knocked her to the floor. The glasses in her hand flew across the room.

"Help," she screamed, scrambling to her feet as he forced his way in. Unable to get to the panic button on the security keypad Jamilah ran toward the phone.

"911, what is your—"

The man moved quickly, simultaneously snapping on a pair of latex gloves and jerking the phone cord from the wall. He yanked her toward him, and clasped his hand over her mouth. She bit down on his fingers and broke loose.

"Son of a bitch," he spat.

Jamilah bolted toward the hall and knocked the potted schefflera over in front of him as he ran after her. The man bounded over the discarded plant and snatched her by the arm again, ripping her blouse. He pushed her into the wall, drew out a 9 mm from a back holster, and pressed the butt of it against the side of her head.

"You're gonna make me do somethin' I really don't wanna do."

On the verge of hysterics, Jamilah pulled at the collar of her blouse as tears filled her eyes. "Please don't hurt us."

"If you cooperate nothing's gonna happen."

"What are you goin' to do with me?"

The door opened and Jamilah breathed a sigh of relief to see that it was Ade, until the man addressed him.

"What the hell took you so long?"

An olive-skinned, raven-haired Latina stepped out from behind Ade with a gun in his back. "Our friend here needed a little more convincing."

Jamilah was confused. "Ade, what is going on?"

He couldn't look at her.

"Get the kid," Jamilah's attacker demanded.

"No," Jamilah cried. "Don't do this."

Ignoring her pleas, the woman forced Ade to the back to retrieve Cerena.

The man shoved Jamilah toward the side door between the kitchen and dining room. "I'm goin' to open this door and the two of us are gonna walk out of here and get into that van." He scanned the area around the house from the kitchen window. "If you so much as blink in the wrong direction I'll drop you like a sack of potatoes, and then I'm gonna put a bullet in the little girl's head. Do you understand?"

Jamilah nodded.

It was two o'clock in the afternoon. Alex had gone grocery shopping and maybe, by some miracle, she'd soon be pulling up with John in tow. Stepping outside Jamilah prayed that Ernie Mae would at least be out watering her prized azaleas, or Margaret would have realized she'd forgotten her glasses and doubled back with Pauline to get them. The mailman was pulling away from the end of the block and never turned around. She could feel her chest constricting.

"I have asthma. I need my medication."

"Shut up and keep moving."

"But, I need—"

"I said shut up."

The man slid open the side door of the van and heaved her inside. He used a pair of handcuffs to secure her to a rail and darted back into the house to see what was keeping the other two. Jamilah jerked the cuffs futilely, only succeeding in bruising her wrists. She closed her eyes, inhaling and exhaling slowing to steady her breathing.

Oh, God, what if something has already happened to Alexandra? she thought. Her heart stopped when she heard Cerena's muffled cries. The van door opened again and the woman stepped inside with the baby's face pressed into her bosom. Ade got into the passenger seat and the gun-toting assailant climbed behind the wheel. He started the van, backed it out of the driveway, and took off up the street.

"Ade, what is going on? Why are you helping these people?"

He sat with his head lowered in shame, not answering.

Cerena resisted her pacifier from the hands of the strange woman and wailed. "*¡Ciérrele pequeña mocosa!*" the woman insisted.

Struggling to breathe, Jamilah tried to inch closer to her, but the handcuffs didn't allow her much leeway. The man driving the van cut into an alley and slammed on the breaks, thrusting everyone forward.

"You shut that kid up or I will!"

"You're scaring her," Jamilah protested. "She needs her mother."

The man leveled the gun toward the baby.

"Give her to me," Jamilah pleaded. "I can quiet her."

"Gil, *no la quiero. No puedo cerrarla,*" the Latina implored.

The man motioned for the woman to pass the baby to Jamilah. Whether out of a latent act of bravery or a foolish miscalculation, Ade clumsily lunged for the gun. The man's reaction was swift and deadly. He cracked Ade in the head.

Jamilah stifled a scream.

"Stop it, Gil," the Latina commanded.

Stunned, Ade fell into the passenger side window. Blood gushed from a gash in his forehead and he leaned forward, whimpering like a wounded hound.

"Try that again, old man, and it will be your last time." The man pulled a bandana from his pocket and covered Ade's eyes before tearing out of the alley.

"Where are you taking us? What have you done to my daughter?"

Veiled behind a large pair of dark glasses, the fiery Latina blindfolded Jamilah and then took out her cell phone and dialed.

"*Dígame.*"

"*Es hecho,*" she responded.

"Were there any complications?"

"Nothing that could not be handled."

Alex pulled up in the drive outside the house and grabbed a couple of bags of groceries from the back seat. Opening the front door with her free hand she was horrified by the sight of the disarray in the living room. She dropped the bags on the floor.

"Mama . . . Mama, where are you?" She ran to Jamilah's bedroom and found her purse lying on her bed; her cell phone was on the table beside it. A knot formed in her throat when she rushed into Cerena's room. "Oh, my God!" Alex went to her bedroom and retrieved her .380 from the bedside table. She then picked up the extension and realized the line was dead.

"Hello? Is anyone home?"

Alex jumped and spun around, pointing her gun in Ernie Mae's face.

The woman hollered, "What in the world happened here?"

"Where's my mother?"

"I don't know. We played cards this afternoon and Margaret said she left her glasses here. I just came down to check. What's goin' on?"

"Get out!"

"What?"

"I said get out, you nosy bitch!"

Alex waved the gun and chased the woman back up the hall and out of the house. She found her purse at the door, pulled out her cell phone, and checked to make sure she hadn't missed any calls; there were none. She promptly called John.

"Mama's gone! They took her! I was out . . . I went to get my hair done . . . I stopped at the grocery store . . . When I got home I found the place in a wreck. They're gone, John."

"Are you in the house now?"

"Yes."

"Is there any sign of forced entry?"

Alex looked around. "I don't know. I can't tell."

"Lock the door, do you hear me?"

"Yes."

"Have you called the police?"

"No."

"Don't do anything until I get there."

Alex picked up the grocery bags and moved them to the kitchen counter. The pitcher of lemonade was still on the table. Some of the condensation from the ice had run down from the glasses and wet the cards that were left just as they had been. She closed and locked the door and set the alarm. She looked at the pot and dirt on the floor but decided not to touch anything. She didn't even want to sit in a chair or on the sofa. It was all too surreal. Still holding on to her gun, she leaned against the arch between the living room and kitchen and sank to her knees.

Racing through the congested freeway with his siren blaring and his dashboard lights flashing, John gave himself a good head start before notifying his superiors. He pounded his fist on the steering wheel. "Rivera couldn't have found her." His thoughts ran to Lorraine, but despite her threats she couldn't have jeopardized his work. It didn't matter now who did what; there was urgency in getting to Alex and getting her out of that house before anything else went down.

It was just after three when he reached the house. He was alarmed to find the police already there. Ernie Mae Hudson was standing on the sidewalk, surrounded by other neighbors, pointing to Alex accusingly. John jumped from his truck and flashed his marshal's badge. The officer blocking his entrance stepped aside. Alex broke from the detective questioning her and rushed to him.

John approached the portly detective. "Hey, Sam, what's going on?"

"We got a call from the woman across the street reporting that Miss Sullivan here accosted her with a gun. I figured I should handle this one personally."

John shot Alex a side-glance.

"When we got here we found the place looking like this. We also found these."

The man showed John an evidence bag of the tracts that were left scattered on the floor.

"We checked around and couldn't find anything else. We questioned the neighbors. Nobody saw anything apparently. Some of them say they weren't even home. Ms. Hudson claims she and two other women who were here earlier hadn't seen or spoken to the victim since about one this afternoon."

"She's not a victim," Alex barked.

"John, I'm gonna have to file a report."

"Look, Sam, can you just hold off on that for a day or two?"

"You know I can't do that. She's not supposed to have a gun, legally or otherwise."

"Did you find a gun, Sam?"

"No. Barney Fife here didn't find a damn thing," Alex interjected. "I wasn't going to let them go through my things without a search warrant."

"C'mon, Sam. Do me a solid. You know how this works."

The detective's face suggested he had a scathing comeback to Alex's sarcastic remark. He rubbed the beard stubble on his dimpled chin. "The only reason I'm even thinkin' about doin' this is because of Hank; you know that right?"

"Yeah, I know."

As the man inhaled and exhaled his rounded belly expanded and contracted. "What about the complaint?"

"Let me worry about that," John responded. "Right now I gotta get her outta here."

"All right. I can give you twenty-four hours, but that's it."

John shook the man's hand. "Thanks, Sam. I owe you."

"Damn right you do."

John escorted Alex back inside the house.

"What did that detective mean when he said the only reason he was doing this was because of Hank?" Alex asked.

"Hank and Sam were rookies together on this gang task force years ago. They got caught in the crossfire of a drive-by. Sam got shot. Hank saved his life. So, they've kind of been looking out for each other ever since."

"I'm sorry I made that Barney Fife crack now."

"So where's this gun that you know is against regulations for you to have?"

"There is no gun."

John's jaw clenched and his brow furrowed.

"I'm telling you the truth. Do you see a gun? Neither did he." Alex reached inside Cerena's playpen and picked up her stuffed rabbit.

"Goddammit! This is my fault!" John snapped. "I gotta get you out of here."

"If Rivera found me here, he can find me someplace else, John. What if that really was him I saw in the club that night?"

"What are you talking about?"

"A couple of weeks ago I went to a club in North Hollywood with a coworker, the night you were at your daughter's dance thing. I saw this man at the end of the bar staring at me. For a moment when the light reflected off his face I thought it might be Rivera."

"Why didn't you tell me?"

"Because, I have been running around for months jumping at every shadow and I dismissed it as just another false alarm. But now . . . it really could have been him."

"Go pack a bag."

"John, I'm not going anywhere until we find them."

He grabbed her arms. "Listen to me, you can't stay here. It's not safe anymore."

She jerked away from him. "It was never safe, John. We were just kidding ourselves. Whatever it takes we have got to get my mother and baby back alive."

"Then let me do my job. Come on, Adriane—"

"Don't call me that! I'm sick of the pretense. For over a year I've been toeing the line and look where it got me. My name is Alex, dammit! Alex!"

John took a step back, rubbed his head, and put his hands on his hips. "Adri . . . Alex, I've got to get you out of here. I promise you I'll do everything I can to find your mother and baby, but I need you to cooperate."

"You promise? Your promises aren't worth shit right now, John."

"Look, I know you're pissed off and you have every right to be, but the more time we waste standing around here, the less time I have to start looking for them."

Alex stared daggers at John before giving in and going to her room to pack. She absently pulled an array of sweaters, blouses, and jeans from her closet. She dumped the contents of her bathroom counter into a bag along with cosmetics and hair essentials; then she removed from under her mattress the .380 she'd hidden from the police, and slipped it in under her lingerie with Cerena's stuffed toy.

"Did you get everything you needed?"

"I don't know. I can't think. It's not like I'm packing for a cruise or something."

John secured the house. While Alex waited in his truck he made his way across the street to question Ernie Mae Hudson again.

"So you're a policeman too, huh?"

"Yeah." John nodded without clarification.

"Well, like I said before I didn't see or speak to Janette since we played cards this afternoon. And I didn't see nobody else. What I didn't tell that other cop was how often I see you parked outside that house."

John overlooked her meddlesome commentary. "What time did you say you came back to your place?"

"It was after one. I needed to be back here so I could watch my stories."

"What about the other ladies?"

Ernie Mae sighed impatiently. "Pauline drove Margaret home. Then about ten or fifteen minutes after two Margaret called me and said she'd been tryin' to get in touch with Janette because she left her glasses. She said she couldn't get through the line so I told her I would come and see. That's when I found your little girlfriend waving a gun in my face."

"Thank you, Ms. Hudson."

"If I were you, I'd be lookin' for that slick-talkin' African Janette was always blatherin' about."

"When was the last time you saw him around?"

"Last night, just after you left. But that don't mean he didn't show up today while I was watchin' TV."

John turned and headed back across the street. He hopped in his truck and reviewed the information sent to his BlackBerry about Ade Obafemi: his picture, his history, his address.

"Where are we going, John?"

"We're going to pay a little visit to a 'slick-talkin' African.'"

Ade's address took them three blocks east of Huntington Street. He occupied the lower apartment in a two-story walkup. John insisted Alex wait in the truck; she didn't. He knocked on Ade's door and called out to him, but there was no answer. Unwilling to leave any stone unturned John pulled out a small tool kit and jimmied the lock. "Stay here," he demanded; she didn't. He cautiously went inside with his gun drawn and looked around. No Ade. No sign of Jamilah. He pulled on latex gloves and picked up framed pictures to examine them, hoping to find any crumbs of a clue. There were pictures of Ade and who he assumed to be his deceased wife among other framed photographs of his family. He sifted through drawers and opened unpaid utility bills, but there was nothing to be found. With the exception of a few dishes in the sink the entire place was clean. After several minutes they exited his apartment and went back to the truck.

"So, that's it? That's all you're gonna do?" Alex questioned.

John's silence was louder than any confirmation. He pulled out his cell phone and called his detective friend.

"Sam, it's John Chase. I need you to put out an APB on a man named Ade Obafemi. O-b-a-f-e-m-i . . . Yeah, I think he may have something to do with all of this. If he's involved he may be trying to leave the state. He's got family in Chicago and Nigeria. I've got his picture. I'll send it over to you . . . Thanks, man."

"What the hell is going on, John? I thought you had him checked out already. How could this have happened?"

John didn't respond.

"Answer me, dammit!"

"I don't know, Alex. I just hope it's all a coincidence."

"Coincidence? My mother and my baby were kidnapped. They could be . . . they could be dead, and all you have to say is this could all be a coincidence!" Alex climbed back into the truck and slammed the door.

"Look, I'm sorry. I know that doesn't mean shit right now, but it's all I got." John slid behind the wheel and drove off. "I fucked up, Alex. All I can do is try to fix this."

He reached out to take her hand. She snatched it away. He shook his head and pulled over to the side of the road. He removed a small USB device from the inside of his jacket pocket and inserted it in the port on his phone. "Do you have your cell phone with you?"

"Yes, why?"

"Give it to me."

"What for?

"Just give it to me."

She took her phone from her purse and he affixed a similar device to it.

"What are you doing?

"Scrambling the GPS tracking. I don't want anybody to know where we're going."

Forty minutes later they pulled up outside a Comfort Inn hotel off Santa Monica Boulevard.

"What if we were followed?"

"We weren't." He held up his phone as a reminder. "I know you're having a hard time trusting me right now, but I'm going to do everything I can to make sure this all turns out right." John got out of the truck guardedly, looking around to ensure that he could substantiate his claim.

Alex grabbed her bag and joined him. They checked into the hotel under the names that they'd used before, Mr. and Mrs. John Carter (John had the identification to prove the alias). Once settled in, John cased the room and its surroundings, particularly the location of the stairwell and how one might easily gain entry to the floor without using the elevator. He found that the door on the ground floor was locked and could only be opened with a key card from the outside or, in the event of a fire, from the inside.

Overwhelmed by the gravity of the situation, Alex held on to the stuffed rabbit she removed from her bag, slumped down at the foot of the king-sized bed, and wept. John eased close to her and took her in his arms; this time she didn't pull away. A tidal wave of emotion collided and washed over her.

"Just when I started to feel like maybe everything was going to be all right. How did I ever let myself believe he would leave us alone?"

"This is my fault," John conceded. "I was careless. I wasn't thinking like a cop. I let this happen."

"I was a distraction."

"No—"

"Yes. I was."

John couldn't raise an adequate argument. "It was more than just you. This shit with Lorraine. I let it all get to me. It threw me off my game."

"And now my mother is paying the price." Alex dried her tears and wiped away the residue of mascara stinging her eyes. She went to her travel bag and dug out a business-sized manila envelope and handed it to him.

"What's this?"

"A couple of weeks ago I got really scared that if something happened to me Cerena would be left alone. So, I wrote a letter to her father. I couldn't mail it. I took it to the bank and put it in a safety deposit box. This is the information to get it out. You know that Betty Ellis is Tirrell's grandmother, and his brother works in the DA's office. Tirrell may not be worth a shit, but I know his family would take care of Cerena. If I die they need to be notified."

"Alex."

"Everything you need is in this envelope. If you can't promise me anything else, you have to make sure Betty Ellis gets that letter. I don't want my baby growing up without . . . without family."

"Nothing is going to—"

Alex pressed her fingers to John's lips to keep him from making any more promises that neither of them was sure he'd be able to keep. "You know who Tirrell is and you know he's in Atlanta. All the information is in my files. Just make sure this letter gets where it needs to go."

"Okay, if it'll make you feel better."

"Nothing is going to make me feel better until we find my mother and baby."

John's cell phone rang as he moved to the window and looked over the perimeter of the parking lot below. "Donovan, what's up?"

"You tell me. I thought you were supposed to meet me at Casey's for a beer."

"Yeah, something's come up. Janette Sullivan and the baby went missing."

"What?"

"I think Rivera got to them."

"What about the girl?"

"I got her out of the house. She's with me."

"Where are you?"

"Out of the line of fire, for now."

"Tell me where you are I'll come meet you. If Rivera's made a move we got to bring the girl in."

"I don't know if that's a good idea."

"John, what the hell are you talkin' about?"

"Right now, I need to make sure Alex stays safe and the only way I can do that is if she stays with me. The fewer people who know where we are the better."

"Alex? You're calling her Alex now? Aw, man. You're really fuckin' up here. I'm your partner. Let me help you make this right."

"Donovan, I gotta go."

"John, wait—"

"I'll check in with you in the morning." John ended the call, cutting Donovan off before he could raise an objection over his handling of the situation.

"Why didn't you tell him where we were?" Alex asked.

"I'm not bringing him in on this until I know what the hell went wrong." He started toward the door.

"Where are you going?"

"I'm going back to the house to look for anything we may have missed that might tell me where your mother was taken."

Alex grabbed his arm. "You can't leave me here by myself."

He loosened her grip. "I won't be gone long."

"What am I supposed to do?"

He glanced over her shoulder toward her travel case. "You know that gun I'm not supposed to know you have? I don't wanna know where you got it from, but if anybody comes here and tries to get in, use it. Don't look at me like that. I'm no Barney Fife. You need to protect yourself; I get that. But you need to be careful with it."

He kissed her and admonished her to lock the door behind him.

It was nine o'clock when John got back to Monrovia. The usually quiet neighborhood had returned to itself. Other than the occasional car passing through, the only noise on the street was the distant bark of a dog. There were still lights on at most of the houses, but Alex's stood ominously dark and still as if to warn of a crime that had taken place there, and maybe even one that was yet to come.

The groceries were untouched on the counter: warm milk, broken eggs. A pitcher of watered-down lemonade was on the kitchen table, a deck of playing cards, a broken lamp, crumpled area rugs, the strewn dirt from the potted plant. Definite signs of a struggle. As he picked up trash and wiped up spills he contemplated what he'd overlooked earlier that would redeem him. He found a discarded tract underneath one of the rugs and stared at it, hoping it would provide an answer. "Judgment Day," he whispered. What was the link? If Jamilah and the baby were still alive he wondered for how long. After securing the house he headed back to Santa Monica.

"Who is it?"

"It's me. John."

Alex hesitated before opening the door. After John dashed inside she locked it behind him. "Did you find anything that could help?"

"No."

"Anything turn up on Ade?"

"Not yet." John dragged into the room, peeled off his jacket, and flopped down in a chair next to the window, rubbing his eyes. "You should try to get some sleep."

"I can't sleep."

"Try."

Alex pulled at the oversized T-shirt she was wearing, walked over, and knelt down in front of the beleaguered inspector. "This is what happens when I let my guard down. I let myself believe that we actually had a future together. The FBI agent and the fugitive. Sounds like one of those cheesy Lifetime movies, doesn't it? Just once I wanted it to be true."

He looked at her with weary regret. She reached up, caressed his head and the stubble on his face. He closed his eyes, breathing in the fragrance of the vanilla bath oils on her skin. She climbed into his lap and kissed the prickly hairs of his neck until her lips found his. Feeling his body's reaction on her bare buttocks, she pulled her T-shirt off.

"Make love to me," she whispered.

"Alex, we . . . Not like this."

Tears pooled in her eyes. "Please."

He took her face in his hands and ran his fingers through her hair. She rose up and led him over to the bed, and he kicked off his shoes, disrobed, and climbed in next to her. Kissing her wet, salty tears, he rolled over on top of her, gently resting the weight of his frame and entered her with measured intensity. He hissed and the contour of her body gradually surrendered to him with every metered stroke.

Alex gasped and cried, "Stop."

"What's the matter? Am I hurting you?"

"No. I can't do this. Not now. It doesn't feel right."

John sighed and pulled out.

"I'm sorry."

"C'mere." John lay on his side and pulled Alex into him. He kissed her softly on the lips. "You don't have anything to be sorry for. There's a lot going on. We don't have to do anything you don't want to do."

"I just need you to hold me."

"I can do that."

John enveloped Alex into his arms and she snuggled close to his chest, breathing in his scent. Secured by his embrace she eventually drifted to sleep.

13

Alex awoke on the verge of hysterics the next morning when she saw that John wasn't there. She threw back the covers, jumped up, and ran to the window. She could see the parking lot but not his truck. Her cell phone rang and she leapt across the bed to answer it.

"Hello . . . Hello . . . Mama, is that you? John? Hello?"

The call ended. She looked to see what number registered; it listed UNKNOWN. Still she hit redial as if expecting it to go through. She spotted a note written on the hotel stationary next to the lamp and picked it up.

Be back soon. Stay inside and keep the door locked.

She grabbed her bag from the side of the bed and checked to make sure her gun was still in it. She then pulled out her undergarments, a pair of skinny jeans, and a sweater, and went into the bathroom. Several minutes later she returned to discover that while she was dressing the unknown caller had called again.

There was a light tapping at the door.

Alex reached for her gun. "John?"

"Yeah."

She put her gun away and quickly unlocked the door. John pushed in, bearing coffee and a bag from a nearby deli. He'd also apparently gone home to clean up and change clothes.

"I got you something to eat."

She forced a smile and took the coffee. "Thank you. But, I'm really not hungry."

"Come on. When was the last time you ate?"

"Um, yesterday afternoon, I think."

He sat down next to her on the bed and opened the bag. "Look, I got bagels and sausage and biscuits. I didn't know what you would have a taste for."

"I don't want anything."

"You gotta eat something."

Her stomach agreed. She jumped when her cell phone rang again. UNKNOWN.

"That's the third time this morning."

John picked it up but didn't say anything right away. He listened, trying to hear background noises. A few seconds passed before he spoke. "Who is this?"

There was no answer.

The woman on the other end quickly pressed the end button on her cell phone. "*Carajo,*" she spat, tossing her long, straight hair.

"Did she answer?" the balding captor asked, entering the room carrying grocery bags.

The woman paced the floor of the sparsely furnished room. "Did you get rid of the van?"

"Of course I did. I know what I'm doin'. But, apparently he didn't think of everything. How long are we supposed to keep them here?"

"We keep them until we are told otherwise," the woman countered.

"I don't like this. I didn't sign on to be some damn babysitter for two old people and a screamin' brat."

The Latin beauty arched her brow, sauntered toward the man, and snatched one of the bags from him. "You are getting paid to do what you are told." She examined the contents of the bag. "*Idiota. Le supusieron traer detrás un inhalador para la mujer. ¡Usted no puede hacer cualquier cosa a la derecha!*"

"Hey, speak English, Pilar. I don't know what the hell you're sayin'."

The woman threw up her hands. "I said you are an idiot. You were supposed to bring back an asthma inhaler for the woman."

"What was I gonna do, pull one out of my ass? You need a prescription for those things."

"You need to call and make sure this gets taken care of."

"I don't take orders from you," the man huffed.

"You work for my father. You work for me. *¿Entiendes?*"

John swiped the card key to the door of his office and went in to find Harley Donovan there alone.

"Where the hell have you been?" Donovan demanded, hanging up the phone.

"I'll explain later," John replied as he sat down to log in to his computer.

Donovan reached over him and placed his hands over his keyboard. "I think you'd better explain now, buddy. Toliver's been askin' about you every five minutes. He's pissed that you haven't checked in or answered his calls, but I've been coverin' for your ass. Hey, remember me? I'm your partner. Whatever you're doin' if it affects you it affects me too. If somethin' is goin' down with this case I need to know about it. You need to start thinkin' with your big head and not with your little one."

John fell back in his chair. "What have you told him?"

"I told him that Lorraine is ridin' you about this separation and you're tryin' to work out custody issues with her. You know the little general is only goin' to buy that for so long."

"You better not let him hear you calling him that."

"No chance of that. He went downtown. So, you wanna tell me what's goin' on?"

"All right . . . Janette Sullivan and the baby were kidnapped yesterday."

"You already told me that."

"I think this Ade Obafemi is mixed up in this somehow."

"What makes you think that?"

"Because he's missing too. I went by his place last night and he wasn't there. I went back there this morning. His bed doesn't look like it's been slept in. Everything looked like it did when I went there yesterday. There wasn't any indication that he'd been there in the last twenty-four hours. No sightings of him at the bus station or the airport."

"Where'd you stash the girl?"

John looked at his partner and then glanced around the office. "I can't tell you that."

"Why the hell not?"

"Somehow somebody found out where we were keeping her and that wasn't by chance. There's a leak somewhere. Somebody is either working for or with Rivera and I'm not telling anybody anything until I get some answers."

"You don't think it was me, do you?"

John pushed away from his desk and moved to the window.

"You're in this shit up to your eyeballs, John." Donovan rubbed his hand over his facial stubble. "You need to tell me where she is so I can help you, buddy."

"I can't do that."

"John."

"Look, Harley. Janette Sullivan and that baby could be dead because I screwed up. I'm not going to let that happen to Al . . . Adriane."

"So, you're just gonna go solo on this? Toliver's not gonna like that shit at all. Your ass is seriously on the line here."

"And if I tell you where she is yours will be too."

"Thanks for the concern, but I can take care of myself."

"Okay. You wanna do something? Help me track down the people who took Janette Sullivan. If we can find them they could lead us to Rivera."

"Where do we start?"

"With Obafemi's daughter in Chicago or his son. They may have heard from him."

"Okay, I'm on it. What are you gonna do?"

"I need to check into something. After that I'm going back over to Monrovia to canvass the neighborhood again. Somebody has to remember seeing something."

Remembering what Alex asked him to do in regard to keeping his promise to contact Betty Ellis if anything happened to her, he logged in to his computer and searched out anything current he could find on Tirrell Ellis. The query turned up information regarding the 2008 shooting that left him paralyzed, and the details that allegedly tied him to Xavier Rivera. He also found the names of Betty Ellis listed as his grandmother and that of his brother Kevin, who was also shot. There was no other mention of Tirrell beyond the shooting, but he did discover that Kevin Ellis was now a district attorney. He deleted his search history before logging off the computer. Examining the envelope Alex entrusted him with, he pondered his next move.

Ade winced as he nursed the gash in his forehead. Jamilah refused to look at him as she cradled a sleeping Cerena in her arms.

"I do not blame you for hating me," he said.

"I asked you not to speak to me," Jamilah snapped. "You have deceived me in the worst possible way. I couldn't care less what you have to say now."

"I didn't realize what was being thrust upon me. I thought you were who and what they told me you were. But, you weren't like they led me to believe at all."

Jamilah sneered. "Who exactly did you think I was?"

"They told me that you and your daughter were criminals. Drug dealers. Fugitives. They showed me newspapers that claimed she was responsible for the deaths of many people. I didn't know there was a baby involved. All I was supposed to do was gain your trust and get close to you in exchange for the wellbeing of my family."

"My daughter is no murderer and neither am I. But, I can't say the same for the people you did all this for. Xavier Rivera. He is the drug-dealing murderer who is after my daughter."

Ade looked forlorn. "They gave me no choice. I didn't know what to do. I needed to protect my family.

"At the expense of my family."

"I was put in an untenable position. I knew this kind of ruthlessness in Nigeria. I brought my family to this country to get away from that."

"So, how did they come to find you, the Yellow Pages?"

"The girl, Pilar. She approached me a few months ago in the very market where we met. I can only assume now that she had already been watching you."

"So, you have proven to be no better than the cruelty you chose to flee. You do realize that these people have no intention of keeping their word." Jamilah held her chest and wheezed and coughed. "Whatever you were promised is all a lie. What would your Busola say if she could see the kind of man you are now? I hope it was worth it."

"Janette—"

"Do not speak to me. Leave me alone."

Jamilah looked around the cluttered room, trying to determine where they were being held. Taking care not to wake Cerena, she stood and walked over to a window that was secured by bars and bolted to a metal frame; wooden boards were nailed on the other side.

Ade went to the window and grunted as he yanked at them unsuccessfully.

Jamilah scoffed. "Where was this demonstration of manliness before you were trapped in this 'untenable position'?"

Pilar unlocked the door and Gil stepped into the room carrying a tray of food and plopped it down on a table. "Eat up," he sneered.

Jamilah glared at him. "I don't want anything from you people."

"It is not our intention to do you any harm, but you need to eat," Pilar injected. "There's a bottle for the baby."

"I don't want anything from you people," Jamilah snapped.

"It is not poison." Pilar picked up a piece of toast and took a bite. "You see? If we wanted you dead you would be already."

"Then what do you want?"

"Your daughter."

Ade cagily watched the man guarding the door. He focused in on the gun in his hand as he moved toward the tray and picked up one of the steaming hot cups of coffee.

"You better not be thinkin' about doin' what I think you are, old man."

Ade slowly raised the cup to his lips, blew, and took a sip.

Cerena stirred in Jamilah's arms and started fussing. "She needs changing."

The man stepped outside the door to retrieve a bag and tossed it inside the room. A package of diapers and baby wipes fell out on the floor.

"You see, we are not barbarians." Pilar's smile was drenched in deception. "I even have a prescription for your inhalers."

"Oh, and how exactly did you manage that?"

"You would be surprised what you can accomplish in this country with the right connections. Or perhaps you wouldn't, after all, that is how you and your daughter were able to assume new identities and go into hiding, is it not?"

She turned and swiftly left the room. The man followed and locked the door behind them.

John reviewed his notes to see if there was anything or anyone on Huntington that he failed to question. When the mailman drove up he glanced at his watch and decided to act on a hunch. As the wiry man stepped outside his truck John flashed his badge. "Excuse me, can I talk to you for a minute?"

"What's this about?" the man asked.

"Do you work this neighborhood every day?"

"Not if it's my day off."

"Were you here about this time yesterday?"

"Yes, as a matter of fact I was."

"Did you deliver mail to this house?"

"Yeah, why? Did something happen?"

"Have you ever seen the people who live here?"

"Yeah, uh, Miss Janette. She's a real nice lady and that daughter of hers . . . Man, I'm tellin' you what. Both of 'em look like they could give you a run for your money, you know what I mean?"

John cut through his mannish amusement. "Do you remember seeing anything out of the ordinary yesterday? A car that you didn't recognize? A truck or van? Anything at all?"

The man pulled his cap off and scratched his thinning hair. "Well, now let me see. I did see a van. It was dark, maybe blue . . . No, I believe it was black."

John perked up. "What else? Can you remember anything distinctive about the van?"

"I remember that it was hanging out in the street enough for me to have to go around it to get to the mailbox. I really hate when that happens. You tell people all the time not to block their mailboxes, but do they listen?"

"Did you happen to catch the number on the license plate?"

"No, but then again I wasn't looking at it. The windows had a heavy tint to 'em, though. Did something happen to Miss Janette or her daughter?"

"Can you tell me anything else about the van?"

The man shook his head. "No, sorry. That's all I remember."

John thanked the man and he turned to grab his mail sack from the floor of the truck.

"Oh, wait a minute. There was somethin' else. The word Christian somethin' or other was stenciled on the side. Maybe it was some kind of old church bus. I couldn't make out any of the other words."

"Thanks. You've been a big help."

John called Donovan to apprise him of the details that he'd gotten from the mailman.

Donovan wiped the residue of cocaine from the base of his nose and pinched his nostrils together and hissed, "Hello."

"Hey, Harley, it's John."

"What's up, buddy?"

"I got a lead I need you to follow up on."

"Okay. What ya got?"

John hesitated. "You all right, man? You sound funny."

"Yeah, my sinuses are actin' up, that's all."

"Where are you?"

"I came home to get some medicine."

"Will you be able to check this out for me?"

"Yeah, yeah. What ya got?"

"I found a mailman who saw a dark blue or black church van parked outside the Sullivan house between one-thirty and two o'clock yesterday afternoon. He said it had the word Christian something written on the side of it."

Donovan sniffed and ran his fingers through his tousled mane. "That's kinda vague, John. You have any idea how many church vans in or around Monrovia that could fit that description?"

"Yeah, I know it's not a lot to go on, but we can at least run a list and see what comes up. I already got Detective McFarland looking into it. If we pool our resources we should be able to narrow it down."

"Okay, I'll get on it when I get back to the office."

"Did you reach out to Obafemi's son and daughter?"

"Just waitin' for a call back."

"Keep me posted."

"You got it, buddy."

Donovan hung up his phone and snorted another line of cocaine from a small mirrored tray that lay on the table in front of him. He tucked his shirt back into his pants, raked his fingers through his hair again, and placed another call.

"Chase is still diggin' . . . No, I got it covered. He doesn't know any more now than he did before. He's so strung out on that girl right now he's about as useful as a pogo stick in quicksand. Don't worry about it. If he gets any real leads you'll be the first to know. In the meantime I'm gonna keep after him to tell me where he took the girl."

14

Alex's pulse quickened when her cell phone rang again. Another unknown caller. She answered it but didn't say anything right away. She listened to the dead air. "Who is this?"

"*Hola mi querida,* Alexandra."

She froze.

"Are you enjoying our little game of cat and mouse?"

"Xavier."

"I'm bored with it myself after all this time. That's why I've decided to accelerate the thrill and make things a bit more interesting."

"What did you do to my mother?"

"Why don't you ask Inspector Chase?"

"What?"

"You are literally sleeping with the enemy. *¿Verdad?* How do you think I knew where to find you? La Bella . . . That quaint little bistro the two of you dined in together . . . The hotel you stayed in after. Oh yes, and then there was that very loud, very crowded nightclub in North Hollywood. You looked positively stunning."

"It was you I saw."

"I just wanted you to know that I was watching, biding my time, waiting for the precise moment to strike.

"You son of a bitch!"

"Poor Alexandra, the men in your life constantly disappoint you, don't they? First there was your father, then your ne'er-do-well husband. Oh, and let's not forget about the progenitor of that adorable little girl of yours."

"What did you do to my baby?"

"Nothing yet. But what happens now is up to you."

Alex's eyes teared up. "What do you want?"

"Well, I'm glad you asked. It's very simple really, I want a pound of flesh. I'll be in touch."

The call ended and Alex jumped when the electronic lock clicked on the hotel room door. She grabbed the gun lying next to her on the bed and cocked it. "John?"

"Yeah, it's me."

Alex thought about what Xavier said and wondered how else he could have known where she was.

"Open the door. I brought you some food."

"Where are they, John?"

"Who?"

"You were in on this from the beginning, weren't you?"

"What are you talking about?"

"That's how Rivera knew where to find us. You played me."

"Who told you that?"

Alex stood with her gun trained on the door and didn't answer.

"Come on, I hope you know me better than that. Look, I don't want to talk in the hall like this. Take the latch off the door and let me in. Alex, I'm not involved in this. I swear on the lives of my children. You have to believe me."

Alex lowered the gun, unlocked the door, and stepped back into the room. John entered, looking around as if expecting to find someone else there. She flinched when he moved toward her.

"Give me the gun. I'm not going to hurt you." He raised the bag in his hand. "See, it's just Chinese."

"You did this. You put this whole thing in motion."

"Alex, look at me. Look at me. Do you really think I'm behind all this?"

Tears streamed down her face. She took a deep breath and guardedly handed over the gun. He promptly removed the clip.

"You heard from Rivera, didn't you?"

She nodded. "He knows I'm here. He knows everything."

John sat the bag down on the bureau and pulled Alex into an embrace. "You're shaking."

"I've never felt so helpless."

"Did he say anything that would give you an indication of where he was?"

"No. But he did say that I was sleeping with the enemy. How would he know that, John? How else would he know where I worked, or about the restaurant in L.A., or the hotel we stayed in that night?"

John pulled away and looked at her.

"What is it?"

"Your best enemies are the ones you don't see comin'. Dammit! How could I be so fuckin' stupid?" John smacked his forehead repeatedly. "I should have known."

"You should have known what?"

"It's Donovan. It has to be Donovan."

"Your partner? Harley Donovan? He's working with Rivera?"

"Him and his dumb-ass good ol' boy act."

"What?"

"Donovan told me that his grandfather used to tell him that your best enemies are the ones you don't see comin'. Rivera said you were sleeping with the enemy. He may have tipped his hand and he doesn't even realize it."

"What makes you think it's Donovan?"

"He found out about you from somebody and it sure as hell wasn't me."

"But why would—"

"I hope to God I'm wrong, but it's the only thing that makes sense."

"What if you're not wrong?"

"Then I'm gonna play his game. If he is mixed up in this I got to make him think he's still in control. It may be our only chance to get your mother and baby back."

Despite Jamilah's attempts to calm her with singing, Cerena would not be placated. Her face reddened and her earsplitting tantrum echoed in the room.

"Shhhh . . . shhhh . . . shhhh," Jamilah pleaded while rocking her and pacing the floor.

"Shut her up," Gil shouted from the other side of the door.

Ade sat contemplatively. Jamilah thought that he almost looked as if he was praying; something perhaps he should have done before ever submitting to the machinations of a monster.

The door flung open and Gil raged in. "I warned you to shut that brat the hell up!"

Ade grabbed the serving tray from the bureau, sending dishes flying, and smashed Gil in the face as hard as he could. Blood sprayed from his nose and he fell back against the doorframe. Ade raised the tray to strike again as Gil rebounded and fired two shots into his chest.

Jamilah screamed and shielded Cerena's face to her bosom. Ade fell backward, clawing at an empty bureau and hitting his head as he sank to the floor. Gil kicked at his body, ensuring he was dead, before turning on Jamilah. "I'm gonna tell you one last time."

A fit of coughing and wheezing overtook her, causing her to hyperventilate.

"Gil!" Pilar charged in and wrestled the gun from him. "¡Estúpido cabron! What the hell did you do?"

"He attacked me," Gil defended. He wiped the blood from his face and held his hand out to her. "Look!"

The chaos was underscored by Cerena's muted cries and Jamilah's struggling for air.

Pilar checked Ade for a pulse. "You killed him?"

"He was tryin' to run," Gil answered.

"You couldn't have just knocked him unconscious?"

"What are we gonna do about the old lady?"

Pilar tucked the gun into the waistband of her jeans and ran cursing into the other room to retrieve an inhaler. When she came back into the room she tossed it toward Jamilah and it landed near her feet. Shaking and clinging to Cerena, Jamilah picked up the device and frantically pumped the medication into her lungs without a second thought. After several minutes she was breathing normally again.

"Are you feeling better?" Pilar asked.

Jamilah nodded as anguished tears flowed and pooled at the base of her neck. "Could I please have a glass of water?"

Pilar glowered at Gil, who had his head back with a rag pressed against his nose. "Get rid of him and clean all of this up," she commanded.

Jamilah turned away, unable to watch Gil carelessly hauling Ade's lifeless body from the room, leaving behind a bloody precursor for what lay ahead.

"Harley, what's up?"

"We found the van."

"Where?"

"It was spotted by hikers at the base of Mount Bliss four miles east of Sawpit Canyon."

John glanced over to be sure that Alex was still asleep and moved to the window. "What about Janette Sullivan and the baby?"

"No trace of them, but Obafemi was inside. He took two slugs to the chest."

"Any word on his family?"

"I finally spoke to his son-in-law. They didn't know what he'd been into here. Apparently his daughter hadn't talked to him in over a week. I'm still trying to reach his son. Different time zones, you know."

"I guess it doesn't matter now."

"Not unless the dead man tells us something."

"I'm more concerned about what the live one has to say," John sneered.

"Huh?"

"Did you find any prints in the van or anything that might tell us anything other than we already know?"

"Forensics is sweeping it now. They're supposed to let me know if they come up with anything."

"Whoever's doing this won't stop until they get their hands on Alex. Maybe it's time to throw out some bait."

"What do you have in mind?"

"Well, it's like yo' dear ol' granddaddy Herman might say, 'to catch rats the cats take off their gloves.'" John disconnected the call and turned to Alex, who had awakened.

"What is it? What's happened?"

"Obafemi's dead."

"Oh, God. What about my mother?"

John shook his head. "No sign of her yet."

"So, what are we supposed to do now?"

"Now it's time to trap a big country-ass, redneck rat."

15

Surrounded by the extravagant spoils of the drug profits he'd secreted away, Xavier Rivera slammed down the telephone receiver and scowled. The strapping Colombian combed his fingers through his now-short bleached mane and clenched his teeth. The unexpected news that Ade Obafemi was dead seemed more necessary than not; still he couldn't afford any more recklessness. Against his better judgment he decided that he would risk yet another return to the States and see to the satisfactory conclusion of this intrigue personally.

He unlocked the drawer of his marble-top desk and extracted his passport. He opened it, looked at the picture, and laughed, rubbing his unshaven chin. He then strode to the French doors on the other side of the large, opulent room and stared out over the picturesque fortress guarding the entrance to Havana Bay, known as the *Castillo de los Tres Reyes Magos del Morro*. He stepped out onto the balcony, sipping a mojito and puffing on a Montecristo cigar, and was calmed by tropical trade winds, contemplating victory. He knew that it was only a matter of time now before Alex resurfaced and he would have his revenge for her treachery.

The soothing sound of the sitar flowed throughout the softly lit exercise studio where a muscularly toned, highlighted brunette whispered, "*Namaste.*"

"*Namaste*," repeated the fifteen other women anchored in the lotus position in front of her.

"Excellent work, everyone. See you all on Friday."

The women whooped and clapped as they moved off the varied yoga mats scattered on the floor and gathered their belongings as they prepared to leave.

Lorraine Chase waved her good-byes, pulled the hood of her fitted warm-up suit over her head, and stuffed her towel and water bottle into her bag. "See you all Friday."

"Aren't you coming to lunch with us?" one of the women asked.

"I can't. I have a hair appointment with Geno in an hour and you know how bitchy he gets when you're late."

She continued out of the building and found Harley Donovan waiting for her.

"Harley, what are you doing here?"

He pushed his sunglasses up on the bridge of his nose. "I'm sorry for showing up like this, Lorraine. It's about John."

"John? What's happened?"

"He's been in an accident."

"What? Where is he?"

"He's been taken to Huntington Hospital."

"Oh my God." She fretfully rifled through her bag for her keys. "I can't remember where I parked my car."

"It's okay. I'll drive you." He took her by the arm and ushered her to his SUV.

"Buckle up," he said, noting her distraction as he drove off.

"Harley, tell me what happened."

"He was on his way to arrest a fugitive who was apprehended in Orange County and he got blindsided by a delivery truck on the freeway."

Lorraine gasped. "You weren't with him?"

He shook his head.

"How bad is it?"

"All I know is his truck was totaled."

"Oh, God."

Her cell phone rang and when she reached into her bag Donovan swerved to the side of the street and pulled his gun. "Let it ring."

Lorraine gasped. "Harley, what the hell are you doing?"

"I'm real sorry about this, Lorraine."

"Have you lost your mind?"

"If you don't do exactly what I say two little kids are gonna grow up orphans. Is that what you want?"

"Where's John?"

"I don't know, but that's what we're gonna find out."

She grabbed the door handle and he hit the electric locks and snatched her by the hair. She shrieked.

"Please don't make me shoot you, Lorraine. We just want John and the girl."

"I don't know what you're talking about. I haven't seen John in days."

"You don't have to know where he is. As soon as he finds out we got you he'll come to us."

"Harley, I don't understand. Why are you doing this? I thought John was your partner. You're supposed to be friends."

"Friends come and go; you just better hope that there's still a little piece of him that cares what happens to you. The people I work with won't give a damn whether you make it home or not."

"What's happened to you? Who's making you do this?"

"The less you know the better. Now, here's what's gonna happen, there's a pair of handcuffs in the glove compartment. I want you to take them out and fasten one end to your wrist, then loop the cuffs through the door handle and secure the other wrist."

"No. I won't do it."

He twisted a clump of her hair around his fist and jerked. "John Michael and little Chloe are gonna be so lonely without you. Now, get the damn handcuffs."

"Okay."

Donovan released his hold and she did what he instructed her to do. Her cell phone rang again. He wrestled the phone from her bag and chucked it out the window.

"Where are you taking me?"

He didn't answer.

"What happened to you, Harley? You used to be a good guy."

"I used to be a lot of things."

"How could you do this to John?"

"It's touching that you still care so much about him, considering he's been screwin' the woman he's supposed to be protecting."

Lorraine looked away.

Donovan put his Bluetooth device in his ear and dialed his phone. "I got her. I'll be there as soon as I can."

They drove several miles before Donovan pulled off the interstate. He extracted an untraceable cell phone from under his seat and attached a device that would distort his voice so as not to be identified.

"What are you doing?" Lorraine asked.

"Upping the ante," he responded. "Not a peep out of you, understand?"

Lorraine sat, terrified, pulling at her handcuffed wrists, resisting the urge to scream for fear of what Donovan might do.

John's cell phone rang as he emerged from the restroom. The call registered unknown. He brushed his hand over his face and head and answered. "This is Inspector Chase."

"Hello, Inspector. How are you this fine afternoon?"

"Who the hell is this?"

"Let's just say I'm a concerned citizen."

"What do you want?"

"You know what we want, Inspector. By the way, did you like that little gift we left you over near the canyon? My associates wanted to set the whole thing on fire but I convinced them it would draw unnecessary attention."

"I assume you called because you want the girl."

"Ding! Ding! Ding! You're pretty good at this. If you liked the first act of this drama wait until you get a load of the finale."

"You know what, I'm gonna find you and when I do that will be your finale."

"That's pretty big talk coming from a man who doesn't know where to begin to look."

"I guess that makes us even, because you have no idea where to find what you're looking for either."

"So, how about we make a trade? We'll give you back your wife if you hand over Alex Solomon. Remember your wife, Inspector? The pretty little redhead. The mother of your children."

John was taken aback by that reveal.

"Are you still there, Inspector?"

"If you hurt Lorraine I swear—"

"That's touching. You had just the right amount of indignation in your voice, too. We'll call you back in an hour and tell you where to meet us. If you double-cross us we'll kill Jamilah Solomon and your wife and then we'll come after your children. Is Alex Solomon really worth all that to you?"

After the call disconnected John dialed Lorraine. She didn't answer her cell, nor did anyone answer at home. "Goddammit!"

"John, what is it? What's wrong?" Alex asked.

"That son of a bitch took Lorraine."

Alex clasped her hand over her mouth.

John removed his standard-issue Glock from his back holster and checked the chamber. "He's gonna pay for this shit!" He charged for the door.

"Wait. I'm coming with you."

"No. You're not going anywhere. Stay here. I mean it, Alex. Don't leave this room."

"I can't just sit around here worrying and not knowing what's going on and losing my mind."

"That's exactly what you're going to do. You have got to trust me to take care of this."

"I'm scared."

"I know you are." John went to the nightstand next to the bed and scribbled something on a pad. He ripped off the paper and handed it to her.

"What's this?"

"It's my stepfather's cell phone number. I really don't want to drag him into this, but right now he's the only person I can trust. If I don't come back . . . If you don't hear from me in the next two hours you need to call him and tell him what's happened. He knows people. He can get you out of here." John pulled the clip of Alex's .380 from his pocket. "Take this. Use it if you have to."

"John . . . be careful."

He caressed her cheek. "I think the time for being careful is over."

John's cell phone rang on his way to his truck. He answered without thinking about it. "Yeah?"

"Inspector Chase, at long last."

"Chief Toliver."

"Well, at least you remember my name. Do you also remember that I'm also the boss?"

"Look, Chief, I'm sorry. I've been meaning to call you. There's a lot goin' on that you need to know about, but I don't have time to talk to you about it right now."

"Well, you better damn well make time, Inspector. I don't know what kind of monkey-ass operation you think I'm running here, but you've got some explaining to do. I got a call from Sam McFarland at the Monrovia PD and guess what tales he's been regaling me with?"

"Chief, I really gotta go."

"I need you to come in and talk to me, Inspector."

"I will . . . later."

"Not later. Right now, John."

"I can't."

"Inspector Chase, if you're not in my office within the hour it's your ass, do you understand me? This is your entire career we're talking about here."

John jumped in his truck and started the ignition. He took a deep breath and exhaled. "Look, Alex Solomon's cover is blown and I have a pretty good idea how Rivera found out. His people took Jamilah Solomon and they took my wife and they're threatening to kill my kids."

"John, where are you? Where is Alex Solomon?"

"I can't tell you that. But, she's in a safe place for now." John looked at his watch. "I'm running out of time. I gotta go." John hung up his phone, threw the truck in gear, and tore out of the hotel parking lot.

He made his way to Donovan's loft and loitered impatiently outside. When someone exited the building he slipped in, bypassed the elevator, and charged up six flights of stairs. He pounded on the door. "Harley, it's me, John." There was no response. John looked around to see if he'd disturbed any of the neighbors. When he realized he hadn't he deftly picked the lock on the door and stole his way inside. Certain there would be something to find he plundered the apartment, turning over furniture and rifling through trash. He scoured every drawer and closet in the kitchen, living room, and bedroom.

While searching through a closet in the bedroom
he discovered an electronically keyed wall safe hidden
behind a row of tailored suits. "Dammit!" John sighed
and wiped his hand over his mouth as he started punch-
ing a sequence of numbers. "Birthday . . . uh, let's see.
March . . . March . . . 030973 . . . 730903. C'mon dammit,
think." Stepping outside the closet John caught a glimpse
of a framed photo on the nightstand of Donovan and his
dog. He thoughtfully rubbed the stubble on his chin and
stared at the picture.

*"Havin' to put my dog down was somethin' I'll never
forget. Somethin' like that stays with you, you know
what I mean?"*

John slapped his forehead. "Son of a . . . Could it be
that obvious?" Rushing back to the safe he held his breath
and carefully punched the numbers 01152005. The safe
clicked and popped open. "Thank you, Bear."

Among other documents that bore the names and
photographs of Gilbert Mosley and Pilar Vélez there was
a passport that Donovan used to travel under the name
Herman Donovan. The safe also contained a stack of
confidential papers that detailed information and dates
about Alex Solomon's allocation into the program. There
were also surveillance pictures of Jamilah and the baby,
and of him and Alex together outside her house, in the
parking lot of the boutique, getting into his car at the
restaurant, and the hotel they'd stayed in while in Los
Angeles. He took the photographs of Pilar and Gil and the
more telling pictures taken of him and Alex; he decided
to leave the rest behind for the police to find. Every shred
of betrayal John uncovered made him angrier. Before the
sun set on this day there would be hell to pay.

16

Situated on a fifty-acre parcel of land twenty miles north of Puente Hills and south of the San Gabriel Mountains, an abandoned farmhouse was veiled by towering California sycamores and teeming with eucalyptus. It was well off the beaten path and could easily be missed traveling most any direction on the interstate to and from the valley or toward the greater Los Angeles area. One had to know it was there in order to find it. The house and property once owned by Harley Donovan's grandparents now belonged to him.

Lorraine had never been so far outside that which was familiar to her and with little sense of direction she doubted if she would be able to locate it again. "What is this place?"

Donovan shot her a side-glance. His silence was unnerving. He pulled up to the house and she noted the license plate of the Land Rover parked in front.

She murmured, trying to lock the numbers in her memory, "2CJC569 . . . 2CJC569 . . . 2CJC569."

"That's not gonna do you any good," Donovan said. "You're not gonna be around long enough to tell anybody."

He got out and went around to the passenger side of his vehicle. He unlocked the handcuffs and pulled her out. Pilar opened the door to the house and stepped out onto the porch. Gil came out and took hold of Lorraine. He leered at her and nuzzled her neck. She squirmed, disgusted.

"Leave her alone," Pilar insisted.

Gil grumbled and dragged her inside.

"I gotta get back," Donovan said.

"What should we do if John Chase shows up?"

"He won't. He has no idea where I am, but I know exactly where he is." Donovan jumped back into his SUV and rolled down the window. "If I'm not back by six . . . kill them."

"What about the baby?" Pilar asked.

"Kill them all." He sped off toward his loft, making ready for the confrontation he knew awaited him.

Gil heaved Lorraine into the room where Jamilah was being kept and locked the door. Both women were startled to see the other. Lorraine stood against the wall, staring warily at Jamilah sitting on the bed holding Cerena as she slept. Jamilah drew up, unsure what to expect next. Lorraine nervously looked around to find a way out without acknowledging her. She tugged pointlessly on the bars at the window much like Jamilah had initially.

Jamilah spoke. Her voice was hoarse and weak. "Unless you have superhuman strength you're wasting your time."

Lorraine turned away from the window and sat on the arm of a ragged upholstered chair facing the bed. She rubbed the bruises left from the handcuffs on her delicate wrists, and caught sight of the trail of dried blood on the hardwood floor.

"How are you connected to all of this?"

Lorraine's eyes fluttered up to Jamilah. "Connected?"

"Are you one of them?"

Lorraine pulled uncomfortably at the neck of her hoodie. "No, I'm not one of them. I don't know who these people are. I was brought here by a man I thought I could trust; apparently I was wrong."

"A man I trusted is the reason I'm here as well."

"I don't understand what any of this is about," Lorraine continued. "What do you think they're going to do to us?"

Jamilah closed her eyes and shook her head, unwilling to give voice to the inconceivable.

"How long have you been here?"

"I don't know. A day or two perhaps."

"Is this your baby?"

"No, this is my granddaughter, Cerena."

"Cerena." Lorraine smiled sadly. "That's a pretty name."

Jamilah caressed Cerena's soft curls and teared up. "It means calm, peaceful, cheerful."

"She's beautiful. I can't imagine that Donovan would do anything to hurt her."

"Donovan?" Jamilah repeated.

"Harley Donovan. He brought me here," Lorraine said. "Do you know him?"

"He's . . . he's Inspector Chase's partner."

"You know my husband?"

"Your . . ." Recognition flashed in Jamilah's eyes. "Inspector Chase is your husband?"

Lorraine's brow furrowed. "Yes. My name is Lorraine. What's your name?"

"Jam . . . Janette Sullivan."

Lorraine gasped. "Adriane Sullivan is your daughter?"

"Yes, she is."

Lorraine stood up and paced the room. "Oh, wow. Now it makes sense. Harley brought me here to get to John. John must be off somewhere with . . . your daughter."

Jamilah looked hopeful. "Then she's all right. She's alive." She cleared her throat. "I think Harley Donovan is working for a man named Xavier Rivera. If the inspector is with my daughter he'll keep her safe."

Both women turned and stared at the door when they heard the key turning in the lock. Pilar entered, flanked by her gun-toting accomplice. She noted the half-eaten sandwich on the tray she'd prepared for Jamilah's lunch. "What was wrong with it? You do not care for the accommodations?"

"I wasn't hungry," Jamilah responded flatly.

"I see." Pilar turned her attention to Lorraine. "Would you care for anything?" Her tone was more condescending than cordial.

"I would care to get the hell out of here and home to my children," Lorraine shot back.

Pilar smirked and removed the tray as Gil stood guard. Seconds later Pilar came back and went to the bed where Jamilah sat, and reached for Cerena.

Jamilah pulled back. "What are you doing?"

"She is coming with me."

"No. I won't let you take her."

"Give her to me!"

Caught between the two, Cerena began to cry. Lorraine looked on, horrified, afraid to move.

"Let her go or I will break her neck," Pilar sneered.

"No," Jamilah wailed as she reluctantly complied. "Where are you taking her?"

"That is none of your concern."

Jamilah struggled upward and lunged toward Pilar as she turned to leave with Cerena. With the baby cradled in her arm Pilar shoved Jamilah backward with her free hand, causing her to tumble to the floor. Lorraine rushed to Jamilah's aid as she clutched her chest and wheezed.

"Please don't take her," Jamilah cried. "She's just a baby. Please don't hurt her."

Pilar swept out of the room and Gil followed, securing the door behind him.

"I can't breathe," Jamilah choked. "I can't breathe."

Lorraine helped Jamilah to the bed and found the inhaler sticking out from under a pillow. She passed it to

Jamilah and she puffed and inhaled the necessary amount of medication into her lungs to settle her breathing.

Donovan drew his weapon and exited the elevator on the floor leading to his loft. He knew at once that the lock on the door had been tampered with. His place was ransacked. His gaze narrowed and he moved cautiously inside. He pushed the door closed behind him with his weapon trained and readied. "John? I know you're here. Come on out, buddy." Uneasily, he opened closet doors, righted furniture, and peered around corners. Continuing into the bedroom he discovered his papers strewn across the floor. He zeroed in on the closet and the open safe. John was nowhere to be found. When he went back into the living room he was startled by the discovery of the front door standing ajar. He crept toward it and stuck his head out to scan the corridor, and was jumped from behind.

John wrapped his leather belt around Donovan's neck and pulled tight enough to cut off his air. Still holding on to his gun, Donovan choked and tried to free himself with his free hand. The harder he fought the more force John exerted.

"Drop the gun," John demanded, kicking the door closed.

Perspiration popped from Donovan's forehead and he flushed various shades of red, but he would not relent.

"I swear to God I will choke the living shit out of you if you don't drop your weapon."

Convinced of the futility of his effort, Donovan ultimately gave in. John booted the gun away from him and let him go. Donovan fell to his knees, coughing and gagging, and John picked up his gun and took aim. "Where are they?"

"Who?"

"No more games. You know exactly who I'm talking about."

Donovan gasped. "Where's Alex Solomon?"

"I'm not fuckin' around with you, Donovan."

"Then don't trade the life of the mother of your children for the life of a piece of ass with a price on her head."

John snatched Donovan by the hair. "Tell me where they are right now or I promise you I'll plug your ass full of lead right here."

"You picked the wrong horse on this one, buddy. If I don't get back to them by six o'clock you'll wish you hadn't."

John racked a bullet in the chamber of the Glock. "I'm gonna count to three and then I'm gonna blow your goddamned kneecaps unless you tell me what I wanna know. One . . . two . . ." He bashed Donovan in the face, sending him hurdling to the floor. "Sorry, I guess I forgot to say three." He pressed the gun to Donovan's crotch. "I just decided your cock would make a much better target."

"Okay. Wait. Wait. I'll take you to 'em."

"Get up."

Donovan pulled himself up and wiped the blood from his mouth with the back of his hand.

John rapped him on the back of his head with the butt of the Glock. "Let's go. And don't even think about trying anything."

Donovan was forced behind the wheel of his SUV and at gunpoint he started for the farmhouse.

"I'm curious . . . How'd you figure it out?" Donovan asked.

"Something Rivera said about enemies when he called Alex. It didn't sit right. I just put it together with what you said before. I didn't wanna believe it until I found the evidence in your safe."

"How'd you figure that one out?"

"You got Bear to thank for that."

Donovan chuckled. "You were always smarter than I gave you credit for."

"Wish I could say the same for you." John extracted his cell phone from his pocket and dialed Lorraine's parents. "Madeline, it's John . . . I'm fine. Listen, can you pick up the kids from the house and keep them with you? Yes, everything's fine. Lorraine's with me . . . I really don't have time to explain right now. I'll have her call you back later. Just keep them with you until you hear from me . . . Thanks, Madeline." He ended the call.

"How do you think ol' Liam and Maddie are gonna feel about you when they find out what you got their little princess into?" Donovan sneered.

"You should be more worried about what's gonna happen to you if anything happens to her," John shot back. "Now keep your eyes on the road."

Donovan chuckled again and glanced over, rubbing the soreness in his jaw. "I think I lost a filling."

"You've been sabotaging this case from the very beginning. You better be glad I don't knock all your damn teeth down your throat."

"Don't you wanna know what happened? Why I . . . turned? Would you believe me if I told you I did this all for love?" Donovan smirked. "Love is what makes the world go 'round, right? Love and lots of money, or love of money. Ain't love the reason you came chargin' in like the cavalry to save the day? I'm not that much different from you, buddy."

"We're nothing alike. And don't call me buddy, you son of a bitch!"

"Oooh, sticks and stones, my friend."

"Just drive, asshole."

During the thirty-five minute drive John took his eyes off Donovan just long enough for him to secure a small can of Mace he'd hidden in the side compartment of the driver's side door just under the handle. He turned off the main road and steered through trees that appeared like sentinels and passed a hefty grove of eucalyptus.

John caught a glimpse of the farmhouse a half mile ahead of them and instructed Donovan to stop the SUV in a tall patch of dried grass. John reached over and snatched the keys from the ignition. "How many are inside?"

Donovan didn't answer.

John pressed the gun into Donovan's temple. "How many?"

"Two."

"Is there a back way in?"

Donovan nodded.

John got out and pulled Donovan's cell phone from his pocket. "Call them."

"What?"

"It's almost six. Call them. Now!"

Donovan reached for the phone with his right hand while he eased his left down to his side to get hold of the can of Mace. He jerked and pointed. The unfocused direction caused the spray to miss its target, filling the cabin with noxious gas.

John's weapon discharged. The bullet shattered the driver's side window. Donovan bolted from the SUV weaving deep into the wooded area. John pursued him. Seeing a clear shot, he took aim and fired. Donovan dropped like a wildebeest.

The echoing blast brought Gil to the door of the farmhouse. John ducked to avoid detection.

Gil stepped away from the house and spied Donovan's SUV. He ran back inside and flung open the door to the room where the women were held. He yanked Lorraine away from Jamilah's side.

"Let go of me!" Lorraine shrieked.

"Your big, bad hubby just showed up for the party." He wrapped his forearm around her neck and kissed her cheek. "Too bad, too. We could have been really, really good friends if we had the time."

Lorraine clawed Gil's bare arm, attempting to wriggle free. The more she twisted the tighter his grip became. A shadow passed across the back window, causing the squirrelly Gil to shoot wildly toward it. Lorraine sunk her teeth into his arm and stomped on his foot. He stumbled backward and tumbled over wood crates that were being used as a table and chairs. John smashed the window with his gun and shot Gil dead as he scrambled to his feet.

John moved swiftly from the window to the door directly beside it as Lorraine unlatched it and threw herself into his arms. "Oh, my God, I'm so glad you found us."

"Are you all right?"

"Yes, I'm fine. John, it was Harley. He's the one who brought me here."

"I know all about it. I handled it." He then stepped over to Gil's body and checked for a pulse. "Is there anyone else here?"

"There was a woman. I don't know where she went, but she took Adriane Sullivan's baby with her." Lorraine turned and pointed. "Janette Sullivan is in there. John, she's very sick."

John followed Lorraine inside and found Jamilah cowering in the corner between the bed and the wall. Despite her weakened condition she was overcome with emotion when she saw John. He slipped his gun back into its holster and went to her.

"John, they murdered Ade," Jamilah cried. "He was a part of all this."

John nodded. "I know."

"That woman took Cerena."

"Can you tell me about the woman?" John asked.

"She was Hispanic," Lorraine injected.

"Her name is Pilar," Jamilah added. "John, you have to get Cerena back before they hurt her."

"I will. I promise."

"Where is—"

"She's safe."

Jamilah cupped his face. Her hands were cold and shaking. "Thank you."

"It's not over yet," John confessed. "I got to get you both out of here. Are you able to stand up?"

Jamilah nodded and gripped his forearm and pulled up. Lorraine moved to her other side to help.

"There's an SUV just up the path." John looked at Jamilah. "Can you make it that far?"

She nodded again, leaning the full weight of her body against him. Her knees buckled when she stepped off the porch and John swept her up in his arms and carried her. Lorraine stayed close.

Sticks and dried grass crunched under their feet as they walked circumspectly toward the SUV. John surveyed the field where he was sure he'd taken Donovan down. Lorraine climbed into the front passenger seat. After securing Jamilah into the back, John pulled his Glock from its holster.

"Where are you going?" Lorraine shrieked.

He ignored her and took a few steps back toward the trail that they'd all just come from. He stopped and listened; there was nothing. No sound. No Donovan.

"John?"

He turned back to the SUV. There was no time to continue the search for Donovan. He needed to get the women to safety. He swept broken glass from the driver's seat, jumped in, and drove off. His thoughts ran to the timeline that he'd given Alex before she was to call his stepfather. He opted to text her instead of calling: No need to call Hank. I found your mother. Everything is all right. See you soon. Stay put.

"That was her, wasn't it?" Lorraine whispered, looking out of the corner of her eye.

Beset by a strange mixture of guilt and accountability John shot her a side-glance. "She needed to know that I have her mother."

Lorraine turned around to see that Jamilah appeared to have drifted off. "What are you going to tell her about the baby?"

John didn't answer. He placed a long overdue call to his chief inspector.

"Inspector Chase—"

"It was Harley Donovan."

"What?"

"He's been in on this with Rivera from the very beginning. You need to get to his loft. You'll find everything there."

"John—"

"I don't have time to get into details right now, but you've got to move on this right now. You should also send a team to this old farmhouse thirty miles west of the Pomona Freeway off Crossroads Parkway South, Route 10; that's where Janette Sullivan was being held."

"Was? John, what the hell is going on?"

"One more thing, Chief; Donovan's been shot. I shot him, but somehow he got away. My guess is it was the woman helping them, or Rivera himself. The woman's name is Pilar Vélez."

"Goddammit, John—"

John disconnected the call before allowing his chief's response. He pulled up outside the entrance to the ER of

Huntington Hospital in less than an hour where he was met by a female attending. Lorraine looked on as they helped Jamilah out of the SUV and into a wheelchair. John took note of the doctor's ID badge.

"What do we have here?" The doctor gave Jamilah a perfunctory spot exam, checking her pupils. "Her pulse is weak. Her breathing is shallow. What happened to her?"

"She suffered a severe asthma attack, and she's most likely dehydrated," John responded.

"Ma'am, I'm Dr. Anderson. Can you tell me your name?"

Jamilah swallowed against the soreness in her throat and glanced up at John. "J . . . Janette Sullivan."

"Ms. Sullivan, are you in any pain?"

Jamilah closed her eyes. "Head hurts."

The doctor stood up to address John. "Are you a relative?"

John showed the woman his badge. "I'm Inspector John Chase from the US Marshal Service."

"Inspector?"

John knelt beside Jamilah and held her hands. "The doctor's gonna take real good care of you. I'm going to take care of everything else. I promise." He stood and gave the doctor a card with Milton Toliver's name on it. "This is the number of the chief inspector of the US Marshal Service Pasadena office." He dashed back to his truck. "Call him. Tell him that Janette Sullivan is here. He'll take it from there."

"Hey, wait a minute," the doctor protested. "You can't just leave her here like this. There are forms . . ."

John sped away.

"Are you sure you should have just left her?" Lorraine asked.

John glanced into the rearview mirror and then pulled over to the side of the road. Wanting to avoid another round with Chief Toliver, he pulled out his cell phone and opted to text him: Just brought Janette Sullivan to Huntington Hospital. In bad shape. She needs protection immediately. Look for ER doc Carrie Anderson. He continued after sending the message, hoping that Toliver would take decisive action.

"I can't believe Harley Donovan was involved in all of this. I was sure he was going to kill me. If you hadn't shown up . . . He threatened the kids, John."

"Are you all right?"

Lorraine rubbed her bruised wrists. "Other than the fact that I might need a rabies shot after biting that man, I'm just a little sore. I just want to get home to John Michael and Chloe. I need to be sure that they're all right."

"I called Madeline earlier and told her to pick up the kids and keep them with her."

John's cell phone continued to ring and text messages kept coming from Alex inquiring about Jamilah and the baby. He only responded to her text telling her to stay put and that he was on his way back there. Once he ditched the SUV and retrieved his truck from the alley two blocks from Donovan's loft he proceeded to take Lorraine to her parents. He called Sam McFarland and told him what happened and asked if he could arrange for a unit from the Pasadena PD to be sent to the Reardon home. His tab was quickly adding up. Milton Toliver called again. John ignored the call. It gave him some comfort to see a patrol car parked on the other side of the street in front of his in-laws' house by the time he and Lorraine drove up.

"I suppose it would be pointless to expect you to come in to check on your children," Lorraine said.

John rubbed his face. "I'll be back as soon as I can."

Tears welled up in Lorraine's eyes and she shook her head. "In all the years that you've been doing this job that you love so much I never felt your family was in danger

until you brought that woman into our lives. You're right . . .
sometimes when something is broken you should probably
leave it that way."

Lorraine got out of the truck and John watched until
she'd made it inside.

Donovan threw his head back, perspiring and cringing,
and pressed the blood-soaked towel against his right
shoulder.

"Try not to bleed to death before I can get you the help
you need," Pilar said.

"I'm just glad you came back when you did," he responded without the slightest hint of the Southern drawl
he'd perfected.

"What the hell happened?"

"Chase got the jump on me. You need to take me back
to my place."

"What the hell for?"

"I've got to clean it out."

"Please tell me you weren't stupid enough to leave
proof lying around for anyone to find."

"Not everything. But it's enough to incriminate me . . .
and you."

Pilar sneered. "*¡Increíble!*"

"Just take me there."

When Pilar pulled up to the intersection of Donovan's
building they could see a squad of agents swarming
around outside.

"My father is not going to be happy about any of this."

Donovan glanced over his shoulder to the blanketed
floor of the back seat. "You took the damn baby, Pilar.
That wasn't part of the plan. What do you think Xavier
will have to say about that?"

"At the very least we still have leverage to draw Alexandra Solomon out of hiding. If you had listened to me

in the first place none of this would have been necessary. You underestimated Inspector Chase. Why do men have to make simple things so complicated? Perhaps my father recruited the wrong agent after all."

Donovan scoffed at the scathing comment. "It's not over yet."

Pilar shot him a side-glance and smirked. "The situation is getting messier and more problematic by the minute. It very well could be over for you."

17

John drove into the parking lot of the Comfort Inn and sat in his truck, staring up at the fourth-floor window. He closed his eyes and braced himself, preparing for Alex's reaction to all that had transpired. His cell phone rang and startled him. It was Alex. He concluded that the only thing to do was deal with it head-on. "Hey, I'm on my way up."

He gave each door a cursory glance as he walked down the corridor toward the room. He rapped lightly on their door.

"John?"

"Yeah, it's me."

Alex anxiously opened the door, grabbed him, and clung to him. "I wasn't sure I'd ever see you again." She inhaled the smell of denim and sweat from his shirt. Just as suddenly and as fiercely as she held on to him she pushed him away. "You scared the shit out of me. Why didn't you answer your phone?" Her gaze narrowed, trying to read the expression on his face. "Where's Mama?" She moved past him and peeked out into the hall. "Where is she, John? You said you had her. You said she was with you."

John took hold of Alex's arm and pulled her back into the room. "Alex, c'mon."

She jerked away; her breathing bordered on hysterical. "Where is she, John? Where's my baby? What the hell is going on?"

"Alex, we need to talk."

Alex shook her head and shoved him. "You lied to me. You said she was with you."

"I didn't lie," John defended. "She was with me."

"Then dammit where is she? Where's my baby?"

"Can you just wait a minute? Your mother had a really bad asthma attack. She wasn't in good shape when I found her. I had to get her to a hospital."

"A hospital? And you just left her there?"

"She's being taken care of."

Alex grabbed her purse from the bed. "You have to take me to see her."

"I can't right now."

"Why the hell not?"

"You know why not."

"John, if they got to her once, they can get to her again."

"No, they won't. Not this time. I notified Chief Toliver—"

"To hell with Chief Toliver. How do you know you can even trust him after everything that's happened?"

"So, what do you wanna do, Alex? Donovan and Rivera are still out there somewhere. You wanna run out of here and go to the hospital and take the chance of being caught or killed?"

"It's better than sitting around here with my head up my ass doin' nothing!" Alex looked into John's tired, haggard expression, huffed, and turned back into the room. She threw her purse onto the bed and screamed, "Goddammit!"

John closed the door, carrying the weight of the day and its burdens in his back and shoulders. With his head bowed he slumped down in a chair next to the bed and pressed the palms of his hands against his face.

Alex turned to him, her face stained with tears. She was eerily calmer. "Where is my baby?"

John shook his head. "I don't know. She wasn't with your mother when I found her. Your mother said a woman had taken her just before I'd gotten there."

"A woman? What woman?"

John pulled out the pictures he'd taken from Donovan's safe and handed them to Alex. "The man's name is Gilbert Mosley, the woman is Pilar Vélez. Do you recognize them? They were working with Donovan." Alex shook her head and eased down on the bed. John continued. "Your mother and Lorraine were being held in an abandoned farmhouse about an hour outside L.A."

"This bitch has my baby?"

John sighed heavily. "I went to Donovan's apartment after I left here earlier. I found these pictures and a lot of other things that proves he's been working with Rivera this entire time."

"He's been watching us?"

"There were other pictures of your mother and the baby. Places the both of you had gone. People you were with."

Alex wiped her tears with the back of her hand. "They took her to get to me, right? They're trying to lure me out and they're going to use Cerena as bait."

"More than likely."

Alex's countenance flashed with hope. "Then she's still alive. She has to be, right?"

John couldn't answer.

Alex combed her fingers through her hair, and paced the floor. "This just keeps getting better and better. I'm so fuckin' tired of being scared. I'm sick of looking over my shoulder, waiting for that son of a bitch to do something else. If he wants me then it's time to give him what he wants. My life for Cerena's life."

"Alex—"

"I'm done with this, John. I need to talk to my mother. I need to hear her voice and see for myself that she's all right. If I can't talk to her then I'm walking out of here and I'm going to find her on my own. I mean it."

John sat pensively and rubbed his hand over his face. "I have an idea."

"What is it?"

He picked up his baseball cap, put it on her head, and stuffed her hair underneath. He handed her his marshal jacket to put on. "Put this under your shirt," he instructed, picking up a pillow off the bed. She looked like a badly disguised heavyset woman. "It won't work," he concluded.

"It has to work," she insisted. "We have to make it work."

John thought more. "Put these on." He handed her his sunglasses. "It's late. By the time we get back to the hospital visiting hours will be over. There shouldn't be too many people around."

"What about guards? If they recognize me they're not gonna let me anywhere near her."

"Let's just go. Hopefully by the time we get there I can think of something else."

Alex slumped down in the cab of John's truck as they made their way to the hospital. John flashed his badge and a smile and engaged in a brief flirtation with a duty nurse in order to ascertain what room Jamilah was in. Slipping into a supply closet he absconded with a pair of scrubs and a discarded lab jacket for Alex to change into. He was glad that Chief Toliver still trusted him enough to have an agent posted outside Jamilah's door. He knew the agent and was sure that he'd been given orders to be on alert for Donovan or Rivera, and most likely him and Alex as well.

"You're going to have to go in on your own," he told Alex. "Cover your face and keep your head down."

"What are you going to do?"

John shrugged. "I'll pull the fire extinguisher if I have to."

Alex started walking toward the room. The hulking agent looked up as she approached. "I need to see your ID," he barked.

Alex patted her pockets and nervously looked around. "Uh, I must've left it in my locker."

"Then you need to go back and get it," the man pressed. "I can't let you in without it."

John stepped up from around the corner. "Hey, Carl, what's up, man?"

"John? What are you doing here?"

John titled his head toward Alex who continued into the room as he distracted the agent. "You're in a lot of trouble, dude. Toliver is mad as hell."

"Five minutes, Carl. That's all I'm asking."

"John, what the hell's goin' on with you and Donovan, man?"

"He hasn't been here has he?"

"I haven't seen him, but both you guys are in some deep shit."

"I know," John conceded. "I had to come by."

"He got your text. He also got a call from this doctor a couple of hours ago. He stormed over here and gave me strict instructions to let him know if you or Adriane Sullivan showed up."

"Carl, man, I need you to do me a solid and cut me some slack. Go get a cup of coffee or something. Nobody has to know."

"That was her, wasn't it? Look, John, I'm not getting my ass chewed out over this."

"Just a few minutes, Carl. Please."

Jamilah's color had returned and her face lit up when she saw that it was Alex behind the disguise. The two embraced.

"Omolola, how did you get here?"

"John. He's right outside."

Jamilah reached out and wiped Alex's tears.

Alex took her hand and kissed it. "This is not the best way for you to spend Mother's Day, huh? I'm so sorry for all of this. If you had died I don't know what I would've done."

"Shhhh . . . I'm right here. And I told you before you didn't get me into anything I didn't know I was gettin' myself into." She pulled tissue from the box on the rolling table next to her bed. "Here, blow your nose. Did John tell you about Cerena?"

Alex nodded.

"Listen to me, she's going to be all right. You can't give up hope."

"We have to be realistic, Mama. Xavier Rivera won't stop coming after me until I'm . . . If we don't end this there will always be another Ade going through you to get to me. I need you and Cerena out of harm's way. If . . . when we get Cerena back I want you to go back to Nigeria and take her with you. "

"What?"

"I'm the one he wants. You don't have to keep this up."

Jamilah ran her hand over Alex's hair and smiled sadly. "I am your mother and I love you. I will never turn my back on you. You are my baby. We stand together, Omolola. Is that clear? When you met Raymond and you got into this drug business I looked the other way. Your father was sick and we needed the money, so I found a way to justify it all. I should have never let you get in this deep. If anyone is to blame it's me."

"Mama, you didn't have anything to do with this. It was my choice to marry Ray and it was my choice to align with Rivera after he died."

"I didn't raise much of a protest to stop you. I will go to my grave regretting that, but I won't leave you."

John tapped at the door and stuck his head inside. "We need to get going."

Jamilah held her hand out, beckoning John to her side. He stepped into the room. "You care for my girl, don't you?"

Alex grimaced. "Mama, don't."

Jamilah scrunched her nose, shook her head, and waved Alex away. "Don't you, Inspector?"

"Yes, ma'am," John whispered. "I do."

"Then you better make sure nothing happens to her."

"I'm doing everything I can."

"Mama, we have to go. I'll try to come back soon."

"John, catch the people who did this, and bring my granddaughter home."

Alex hugged and kissed Jamilah good-bye. John thanked the agent guarding the door on the way out and asked him for his discretion. Instead of chancing the elevator, they took to the stairs.

Anguished tears streamed down Alex's face as they made their way back to the hotel.

"This may not be a good time to tell you this, but I looked up Tirrell Ellis," John offered.

"What did you find?"

"Not a whole lot since his shooting a couple of years ago. His brother's a DA now. There was some mention of his grandmother."

Alex wiped her face in the palms of her hands. "I'm pulling you deeper and deeper into this mess."

Thinking about Hank's forewarnings, everything Lorraine had said, and all that it was costing him John tried to sound reassuring. "You're not pulling me anywhere. I came into this with my eyes open. Besides, my days as a marshal may be over, but I could always go back to school and get that law degree. Who knows, I could be the next Johnnie Cochran."

Once they got back to the hotel John announced that he was going to take a shower. He stripped out of his clothes and disappeared into the bathroom. Alex sat staring at her cell phone, willing it to ring, hoping for any word on Cerena. Every nerve ending in her body tingled with thoughts of the inevitable. She needed relief from the stress that consumed her. She took off her clothes, went into the bathroom, and stepped into the shower. John washed the soap from his face and smiled. The only thing Alex wanted at that moment was to have him inside her. She brushed up against him and the water cascaded over their bodies.

"Are you sure?" he asked.

"We may never get another chance," she responded.

John brushed her wet hair away from her eyes and cupped her face. "I'm going to find your baby, and I'm—"

"John—"

"Let me finish, all right? I'm gonna get you out of this. When this is all over you'll be on your way to a new city with a new identity and you'll have a chance to start over again."

"I don't want to have to start over without you."

They stared a silent knowing into one another's eyes as the water pelted them like rain. John pulled Alex into him and kissed her passionately. She felt the swell between his legs. He gripped her buttocks and pressed her into the tiled wall, licking and sucking her yielded breasts. She wrapped her arms around his neck and opened up, allowing him inside her, fulfilling a yearning and momentarily masking heartache. It was an extraordinarily poignant moment. Her body was imbued by his fervor. Neither could be sure what lay ahead, but they knew they were connected and they would face triumph and even death together.

18

Alex awoke the next morning to find that John wasn't there. She found breakfast on the desk in front of the bed along with a note.

Had to go in. Needed to see Toliver. Got to have help. Be back soon.

Milton Toliver's ruddy complexion flushed a blistery shade of crimson informing of his demeanor when John stepped off the elevator into the marshal's office. "Well, look who decided to finally show up. My office. Now!" John went ahead of his lanky, balding boss. He followed and slammed the door behind them. "Do you have any idea how much shit you've caused?"

"Yeah," John answered. "I have a pretty good idea."

"What the hell, John? Two of my best inspectors are running amok. I got two dead guys, and a missing baby. Give me one good reason I shouldn't lock you up right now. Where the hell is my missing witness?"

"She's safe."

"Safe? That's all you've got to say?"

"I'm not ready to tell you where she is."

"This isn't a request, Inspector. You're a United States marshal. You've broken at least a half a dozen regs that I know of, if not more. You're thumbing your nose at policy and procedure. Just what the hell do you think you're going to accomplish?"

"I need to finish this, Chief."

"It is finished, John. At least it is for you."

"No, sir, it's not."

"This Lone Ranger shit isn't going to cut it anymore, John. The Department of Justice is all over this thing."

"I didn't know who I could trust," John responded. "I still don't."

"You're not referring to me, are you, Inspector?"

John's lack of response was answer enough.

Infuriated, Toliver leaned back in his chair and shook his head. "I don't even know what to say to that."

"Say you'll give me the time I need to figure out where Donovan is hiding out."

"Why the hell would I do that?"

"Because I know him. I know how he thinks."

"You apparently don't know as much as you think you do, otherwise, he wouldn't have been able to get by you for so long."

"Donovan fooled us all. Including you, sir."

Toliver could not deny that aspect. "If I were to give you more time how exactly do you intend to go about flushing him out?"

"They still don't have Alex Solomon. Rivera didn't go to all this trouble slipping back into the country and watching her and following her for nothing. He took his time; that's why he took her mother and baby. He's a sociopath. He wants her to suffer. If he simply wanted her dead he's had more than one opportunity to kill her. We can use his arrogance to our advantage."

"So, what are you suggesting? We just wait for him to make his next move? You got lucky this time. You were able to get your wife and Jamilah Solomon out of this alive, but what if your luck has run out; what then?"

"You can't pull me off this case. I gotta . . . I need to do this. Please, I can't trust anybody else with this. Look what's already happened."

"I'm curious, what was it that got you on to Harley Donovan in the first place?"

"It was something I remembered him saying about enemies."

"Shit." Toliver leaned into his desk and folded his hands in front of him. "You're holding on to this case like a dog with a bone. Is it just because of Donovan, or is there something else you're not telling me?"

John looked directly into the chief inspector's eyes. "That son of a bitch worked with me for five years. He called himself my friend. He's been to my house . . . around my kids. He kidnapped my . . . I want him, and I want him to pay."

If Toliver suspected more he didn't ask. Whatever he may have heard or thought he knew about John's involvement with Alex Solomon he didn't question. He grunted and shook his head. "I spoke to your wife last night."

John tensed up, wondering what Lorraine may have said.

Toliver picked up a file from his desk and tossed it over in front of John. "Based on the description we got from her and Jamilah Solomon, and the evidence we found at Donovan's place, I did some digging. There is something you may find interesting . . . Pilar Vélez is Rivera's daughter."

John perused the file and studied the woman's picture. "Donovan told me that he had done all of this for love and money."

"As far as we can establish they've been travelling in and out of the country together under assumed names for the better part of a year. There are dates on the documents you found that coincide with all the time Donovan had taken off going back to the beginning of 2009. The doctored passport tracked half a dozen or so trips into Cuba and a place called *Castillo de los Tres Reyes Magos del Morro.*

There is a villa deeded to a Marisol Yelina . . . formerly Marisol Vélez. She was Pilar Vélez's mother."

"Was?"

"She died giving birth in 1981."

"Why didn't she show up in any security checks on Rivera before now?"

"I'm still trying to find that out. But, what we do know is that Pilar Vélez grew up in a convent just outside Santa Clara. There was no record listing Rivera as the father. Until you found her papers in Donovan's files she didn't even register a blip on the radar."

John rubbed his chin curiously. "Is Rivera at this *Tres Reyes* place now?"

"Honestly, we don't know where he is," Toliver responded. "I've been in touch with ICE, Immigration and Customs Enforcement, and given them everything we've got. I'm waiting to hear back from them."

"What about the authorities in Colombia or Cuba?"

"Diplomatic relations between the US and Cuba are still sketchy at best. So far I'm not getting dick from the Colombian authorities."

"So, why are you telling me all this?"

Toliver exhaled deeply. "As much as I hate to admit it, you were right. I need you to stay on this. It's too dicey to bring anybody else in. We're moving Jamilah Solomon out of the hospital and into an undisclosed safe house. Rivera's got to be getting pretty antsy right about now. Stay close to Alex Solomon. If that baby is still alive the best chance we have for getting her back is for them to try to contact her again."

John scooped up the file. "Thanks, Chief."

"John, I'm disappointed that you felt you couldn't confide in me. I'm going to bat for you on this. I need you to trust me from here on out, whatever happens; understand?"

John lowered his gaze and nodded affirmatively.

19

The US Customs officer closely examined the declaration form and inspected the passport photo as he took note of the towheaded man in the dark blue pinstriped tailored Versace suit. This was a familiar process that the swarthy Xander Rivers had all but memorized. Simple detailed facts: name, birth date, street address, country of residence, countries visited, and what if anything you were declaring. He didn't even break a sweat knowing that his papers would be found in order and there was no reason for anyone to suspect otherwise.

With one last glaring eye and nothing that remotely resembled a smile the customs officer waved Rivera through. He donned his sunglasses and sauntered arrogantly past security. In a matter of minutes he'd made his way through the Los Angeles International Airport concourse to a waiting Town Car. The driver helped with the one bag he carried and he stepped inside to find Harley Donovan. He smiled warmly. They embraced and Xavier pulled him into a kiss.

"I've missed you, *querido*."

"God, I've missed you too. And I'm glad I can finally drop this *Hee Haw* act."

"An Oscar-worthy performance to be sure. And no one, not even the intrepid Inspector Chase, was the wiser."

They kissed again, more passionately than before.

"I'm glad you came," Donovan continued.

"I had to, didn't I? You and that daughter of mine were making it difficult for me to maintain my distance." Rivera reclined in the plush leather seat as the car motored away from the terminal. "This is taking much longer than I anticipated. But, I must say I am enjoying the risks."

"I didn't expect John Chase to become so uncontrollable."

"Indeed, *Señor* Chase has become quite the fly in the proverbial ointment, hasn't he? I suppose he's not completely to blame in all of this. The beguiling *tentadora* need only to bat her lashes to have a man fall at her feet in service."

"Not every man." Donovan leered.

Xavier kissed his hand and smiled. "Have our other plans been solidified?"

Donovan pulled papers from his jacket pocket and passed them to Xavier. "We'll drive across the border into Mexico. The documents we need will be waiting. From there we'll fly on to Argentina."

"Excellent." Xavier brushed his fingers over Donovan's lips. "You look tired, *querido*. How are you feeling?"

"I got the shoulder taken care of. It looks a lot worse than it actually is. Good thing I'm left-handed."

"It's too bad you didn't eliminate Lorraine Chase when you had the opportunity."

"She isn't the one John loves . . . not really."

Xavier pulled Donovan into another kiss. "Love is indeed a powerful motivator, is it not?"

"Yes, it is."

"No matter, we have the child. And I trust the next time Inspector Chase gets in your way he won't walk away unscathed."

"You can count on it."

***

"Welcome back to the Four Seasons, *Señor* Rivers. Will you be staying with us for a while this trip?"

"Thank you, Scott. It all depends on how quickly I can wrap up my business and tie up loose ends."

Xavier slipped the concierge a one hundred dollar bill, winked, and breezed on to the elevator with Donovan in tow. They rode to the twelfth floor where they found Pilar waiting for them in the suite.

"*Papá.*"

"*Mi hija.*" He smiled. They embraced. Xavier let Pilar go and turned to retrieve a cognac that Donovan poured for him. He unbuttoned his jacket and eased down on a plush chenille sofa facing them and slowly sipped. "Where is the child?"

"Sleeping in the next room," Pilar answered.

"Well, it seems that we have a lot of cleaning up to do, don't we?"

Pilar and Donovan eyed one another.

"I had hoped that all the planning I did would have produced better results by now. I suppose I could walk away, simply disappear, but I do have a reputation to salvage, don't I? Pilar, *quiero que llames a nuestro pequeño problema.* Use pictures of the little one to get her attention. *Querido,* you will reach out to your friend the inspector, but first you will see to the matter that we discussed on the way here. Once the two are separated I will take it from there. I want to be able to look into the eyes of Alexandra Solomon when I do."

20

Outside the Reardons' home everything appeared normal. Nestled among the other affluent homes on Hillcrest Avenue it was the safest place that John felt his family should be until Harley Donovan was apprehended.

Lorraine knocked on John Michael's bedroom door. He didn't answer. She opened it to find him lying in bed on his back tossing a basketball into the air.

"Sweetie, do you think you should be doing that? You just got your cast off."

He didn't respond.

"We're all downstairs about to have lunch."

"I'm not hungry."

"So, he can speak." Lorraine stepped into the room and sat on the bed next to him. "Are you feeling okay? Is your arm hurting?"

"No."

She reached out to feel his forehead.

He pulled away and turned over. "I'm not sick."

"What's wrong?"

"I'm sick of bein' in this house. I wanna go outside and play."

Lorraine threw her head back and sighed. "Honey, we talked about this. I thought we agreed that you and Chloe are better off staying inside for now."

"Please, Mom. Can I please go outside for a while?"

"I'm sorry, John Michael. Until we hear from your father you're not going to be able to, that's just how it has to be."

"Why can't you tell me what's goin' on? Why is that cop hangin' around? I heard you and Grandma Maddie whispering about him. I know he's not really one of Grandpa's friends."

"Your dad . . . your dad just wants us to be safe."

"From what?"

Lorraine didn't answer.

John Michael pressed on. "Dad's never comin' home, is he?"

Lorraine was doing all she could to shield her children from the potential danger they could all be in given what she'd just been through. John Michael was having none of it. He sat up and tossed the ball across the room. It hit the wall with a hard thud, barely missing a window.

"John Michael, you know better than that."

"I hate being stuck in the house. I wanna go outside."

"I said no."

"It's not fair," he pouted.

Lorraine furiously rubbed her temples. "I know you can't fully understand why we have to do what we have to do right now, but I promise you that things will get back to normal soon."

"When? How long are we gonna have to stay here?"

"Let's just give it a few more days, all right?" She stood up and walked back toward the door. "Are you coming? We're having tacos. I know how much you like them."

John Michael turned away from her and crossed his arms in protest.

"Okay. If you get hungry we'll be downstairs."

As soon as Lorraine was out of the room John Michael dashed to the window and slowly raised it. He straddled the windowsill and carefully scaled the lattice attached to the house. It was something he'd done before when he and his sister were left in the care of their grandparents and hadn't been caught. Once he reached the ground he looked around to see if he'd been spotted, and took off up the street, where he hoped to find his friends playing basketball. When he rounded the corner at the end of the block he was disheartened to find that none of them were there. He decided that he'd go to one of their houses just as a dark sedan pulled up to the curb and the tinted window rolled down.

John Michael's face lit up when he saw who the driver was. "Uncle Donny!"

"Hey, buddy. I just circled the block hopin' to see you. This must be my lucky day."

Alex was agitated pacing the floor of the hotel room, waiting for John. It seemed to be the only thing she did of late. Her fate, her choices, her decisions all taken from her and it made her crazy. It didn't help that she was in the throes of PMS: swelling, wild cravings for sex and food, irritability, crying jags, and the ever-attractive constipation. This was not the time or place for nature to conspire against her as well as everything else.

She had just spoken to Jamilah, and it at least made her feel better to know that Milton Toliver had taken her out of the hospital and she was being kept in a place she was sure that Xavier Rivera wouldn't dare try to get at. But, he was still out there . . . with Cerena.

Staring at her cell phone her mind raced again to the unthinkable: what would happen to her baby if she died? She scrolled through the contents of the phone and located Tirrell Ellis's number that she managed to commandeer before her old phone was confiscated. She configured the cell phone so she wouldn't be identified, and dialed, not knowing what she would say if he answered.

"Hello."

Immediate tears flooded her eyes at the sound of his voice. Her breathing intensified. She opened her mouth to speak but nothing came out.

"Hello."

She ended the call, tossed her phone on the bed, and decided to take another shower. While in the bathroom her cell phone rang. After several minutes she emerged to discover that a picture message of Cerena had been sent. "She's still alive." Her cell phone rang again, giving her a start. "John?"

"Guess again."

Alex hesitated. "Is this . . . Pilar?"

"I see you know who I am. I assume you received the picture I sent?"

"Where is my baby? Is she all right?"

"For now."

"If you hurt her, I swear—"

"You really aren't in any position to make threats. But, if you want to see your daughter alive again you will do exactly what you are told."

Alex could hear Cerena's cries in the background. Her heart broke. "What do you want me to do?"

"Are you familiar with the Santa Monica Pier?"

"I know where it is."

"Are you close?"

"Close enough."

"You will need to come to the south end of the boardwalk in an hour, and you will need to come alone."

"How will I find you?"

"I'll find you."

"Will you have my baby with you?"

"We have eyes everywhere. I will know once you arrive at the promenade. If you are not alone, or if the police or John Chase are with you, you will never see the child again. *¿Entiendes?*"

"Yes."

"One more thing for you to keep in mind, *chica,* if you do not come alone you will not only put your own child in jeopardy; Inspector Chase's children will be in danger as well."

When the call ended Alex rummaged through papers on the desk and found the photograph of Pilar. She then grabbed a pair of jeans from her bag and became increasingly frustrated pulling at the fastener and trying to zip them up. She threw on one of John's T-shirts, his windbreaker, and the cap she'd disguised herself with to get in to see her mother. She grabbed a pair of sneakers, pulled her .380 from under her pillow, and headed for the door. Just as she opened it she was alarmed to find John there.

"Where are you going?"

"I don't know. I got to get out of here."

John nudged her back inside the room. Undaunted, Alex pushed her way back toward the door.

"Alex, what is it?"

"What the hell do you mean, what is it? I've been cooped up in this damn hotel room for days. I need to get some air, John. I need to . . . to find . . . I need to . . ."

John held up his hands to her. "Slow down, okay? I know how hard this has been on you, but I can't let you go out there on your own like this. Look, I got a couple of calls from Lorraine and I need to go check on my kids, but when I get back we can go down to the pier, grab some food, and take a long walk."

"Aren't you afraid somebody will see me?"

"No more so than you going out there by yourself."

"John, I—"

John's cell phone rang. "Lorraine?"

She was hysterical. "John Michael is gone."

"What?"

"He snuck out of the house. He was in his room and he wanted to go outside to play. I told him no. When I went back to check on him he was gone."

"How the hell did he get out?"

"He went out the window. We've looked everywhere. I checked with the neighbors and nobody saw him. He's gone, John. Somebody took him. It had to be Donovan."

"Where is Officer Malone?"

"He's still out looking for him. John, what are we going to do?"

"Lorraine, just calm down."

"Calm down! Our son is out there God knows where and you're telling me to calm down! You need to find him, John! No one else in the world should be more important than that, and if you think they are then you're not the man I thought you were."

"Lor . . . Hello . . . Hello . . . Shit," John spat.

"What's wrong?" Alex asked.

"John Michael's gone. He could be . . ."

"No," Alex gasped.

John fought the tears that were welling up. "Let's go. You're coming with me."

"What?"

"I'm not leaving you here, Alex."

"Lorraine will go ballistic if she sees me with you. I don't want to make this any harder for you than I already have. I can't go. Not for this. This is your family. You have to go. I'll be all right." Alex presented the .380 for emphasis. "I'll be all right."

Tacit emotions raged. Alex too resisted the urge to cry. "Go get your son."

Enough was enough. Alex thought as she considered the trap she might be walking into as John bolted from the room. She had to give her life for Cerena's; it was the only way to end this. Now more than ever she was keenly aware that she also needed to give something back to the man who'd sacrificed his own family for hers. She rushed to the window and watched him tear out of the parking lot.

Inhaling and exhaling slowly, she harkened back to the woman she was before any of this happened; the less-fearful Alexandra Solomon checked her gun, composed herself, and prepared to march further into hell and give the devil his due.

21

John weaved in and out of traffic on the 10 struggling with his obligation to his family and his duty to protect Alex; but it wasn't just duty that drove him now. In all the cases he'd worked over the years he was not so profoundly affected before, and the personal stakes had never been as overwhelming.

His cell phone rang.

"Officer Malone just called," Chief Toliver barked. "Where are you?"

"I'm on my way to the Reardon house."

"Where is Alex Solomon?"

John took a deep breath. "She's . . . She's at the Comfort Inn off Santa Monica Boulevard near the pier. Room 412."

"You left her alone?"

"It's not like I wanted to. I had to."

"Goddammit, John!"

The call waiting signaled another call. UNKNOWN registered on the ID. John abruptly disconnected from the chief.

"Hey, buddy, what's up?"

The sound of Donovan's drawl sent a torrent of fury down John's spine, causing the hairs on his arms and the back of his neck to stand on end. "You son of a bitch. Where's my son?"

"Tsk, tsk, tsk, tsk, tsk, Johnny boy, what have I told you about name-callin'? I see John Michael's arm is all better since his cast was removed. It'd be a shame for him to have to break the other one."

"If you do anything to hurt him I swear I will hunt your sorry ass down and I will kill you."

"Choosing your family over Alex Solomon was the right decision, John. But you're runnin' out of time. Tick tock, buddy."

The tires of John's Ram pickup skidded to a stop. He bolted into the house past the policeman assigned to his family to find Lorraine with her mother holding on to John Michael.

Lorraine wiped her tears. "He just walked in right before you got here."

"Where's Chloe?"

"She's in the family room with Daddy," Lorraine answered.

John stooped down and called his son over to him. He embraced him and brushed his hand over the boy's bushy head of hair and checked him out. "Are you all right, John Michael?"

"Yes." He nodded.

"You really scared us, you know that? Why did you sneak out?"

"I just wanted to play and then I saw Uncle Donny and he wanted to take me to get ice cream."

"Why didn't you ask your mother? Didn't you think that she'd be worried that you just took off like that?"

John Michael shrugged.

"Did he hurt you?"

"No. He said he wanted to celebrate me getting my cast off. I'm sorry I scared you. Am I in trouble?"

"Don't you ever do anything like that again, do you understand? And if you see Uncle Donny again you tell me or you tell your mother, am I clear?"

John Michael nodded and lowered his gaze.

John hugged him and kissed the boy's forehead. "I love you, you know that, right?"

The boy nodded again.

John stood up. "Why don't you go into the family room with Chloe and Grandpa. I want to talk to your mom."

The boy looked at his mother. She pressed her lips together and nodded. He scampered off.

"You don't have anybody to blame for this but yourself," Lorraine snapped. "If anything would have happened to him—"

"Nothing happened."

"This time, but what about next time?"

"There won't be a next time."

"Are you sure about that? Can you guarantee that Harley Donovan won't be coming after me or my children again?"

John's cell phone rang. "Chief Toliver, I can't talk right now. I—"

"I just got to the Comfort Inn. Alex Solomon isn't here."

"Dammit!"

The late afternoon Southern California sun was giving way to dusk over the Santa Monica Pier jutting out over the beach, offering a spectacular view of the Pacific Ocean. The prominent one-hundred-year-old landmark was teeming with the excitement of adults and children alike. The smell of popcorn dripping in butter, corndogs, hamburgers, beer, and salt water assaulted her senses, but Alex remained singularly focused and made a beeline toward the boardwalk. The festive music playing meant to amuse and entertain seemed a taunting and vicious underscore to the chill of foreboding that shrouded her. She tucked loose hairs under her cap and kept one hand in her jacket pocket with her finger close to the trigger of the .380. The overexcited beat of her heart sounded like tribal drums with each step. Dodging a vending cart of balloons she bumped into a towering gray-haired man, knocking his tackle box out of his hand.

Alex apologized. "I'm so sorry."

"No harm done," the man responded as he stooped to pick up the contents of the box. "I got it." He looked up into Alex's face and spied the monogrammed J. CHASE on the windbreaker. "Are you all right?"

She fumbled to put on sunglasses. "I'm fine. Just in a hurry." With that she turned and took off.

The man paused, scratching the salt-and-pepper whiskers of his chin and watched her. After collecting his gear he pulled out his cell phone and dialed. "John, it's Hank."

"Yeah, Hank."

"I think I just ran into that woman you're supposed to be keepin' an eye on."

"What? Where?"

"I'm down at the pier . . . John, you there?"

"Hank, are you sure it was her?"

"Pretty sure. She favored that picture you showed me. And she was wearin' a jacket with your name on it."

"Where is she now?"

"Looks like she's headed toward the harbor."

"Hank, you gotta do me a solid and go after her."

"What?"

"She's in trouble, Hank. I'm on my way from the Reardons', but I'm not going to be able to . . . Hank, you gotta help me out here."

Hank sighed. He felt an "I told you so" rising up but he didn't say it. "I'll do what I can."

He gathered his fishing gear and navigated through the crowd several yards behind Alex. Fear flooded into her face when she glanced over her shoulder and noticed him gaining on her. Her pace quickened. She changed directions and blended into a group of tourists moving toward an enormous Ferris wheel. Hank lost sight of her and stopped and turned aimlessly in a circle, trying to determine where she'd gone. He started toward the boardwalk, curiously staring at every female he passed.

Milton Toliver and the female agent who had gone to the Comfort Inn in search of Alex rushed in just west of Pacific Park and got hemmed up in the carnival atmosphere. He frustratingly scanned the hundreds of faces that blurred together. "Dammit, where is she?" He directed the agent go one way and he rushed off in the other.

Alex peered from around an abandoned arcade and spied Hank approaching the crest of the boardwalk and making a call. Was he contacting Pilar? She rubbed her fingers together and put her hand back in her pocket, touching the gun as if to make sure it was still there. If it came down to it, would she have to kill this man in order to get to her daughter? Certain he was looking for her; she waited and watched as he walked up the boardwalk and back. Her cell phone rang and she jumped. It was John. She didn't answer. When she looked up again she didn't see the man who was following her. Cautiously she crept away from behind the arcade and continued. There were women of every nationality milling around, none who looked like Pilar, and none who had her baby. Alex's anxiety escalated. What if Pilar wouldn't show? What if the man who was tailing her was meant to bring her to Cerena? She reconsidered keeping John out of the loop. When she reached for her cell phone she felt what appeared to be the barrel of a gun in her back. Dressed like any other angler on the pier it was easy for him not to be noticed.

Alex gasped.

"Don't scream. Don't turn around. I was beginning to think that you stood me up."

"You took a huge risk coming here," Alex said.

"No more than the risk you took, *mi pequeña flor*."

"You had your freedom, Xavier. As far as anyone knew you were a ghost, you could have just stayed that way. You did all this just to kill me?"

"I did all this to watch you squirm. Admittedly it would have been much easier to have someone do it for me, but what would have been the fun in that?"

Alex did her best to control her accelerating panic. "Just like the fun you had when you had my cousin Bobby killed and when you tried to kill Tirrell Ellis."

"If I had my way *Señor* Ellis would be dead now, but I suppose you'll do in his stead."

"You won't get away with it, not with all these people around."

"My dear Alexandra, I've been practically right up under your inspector's nose for over a year thanks to some very strategic assistance. What makes you so sure I'll be caught?" Xavier patted the pockets of Alex's jacket and removed her cell phone and gun. "You didn't really think I wouldn't check, did you?"

"Where's my baby?"

"She's in very good hands. I assure you that my Pilar is quite capable. It's poetic, don't you think? My daughter becoming a mother to your daughter. I suppose that would make me Cerena's *abuelo*." Xavier chuckled. "*¿Qué delicioso, no? Mi última venganza;* raising the child of the two people who tried to destroy me."

"Funny, you don't seem like the grandfatherly type," Alex scoffed. "And you have lost what's left of your mind if you think I'm going to let you do this. I will fight you with everything in me to keep that from happening."

"Let me? You seem to think you have a say."

"You can't kill me here."

"I have no intention of doing anything here. Do you see that sedan that just pulled up over there between the pizzeria and that hot dog vendor? Why don't the two of us take a nice little stroll toward it?"

"If you're going to kill me I need to know that my baby is going to be all right. Please let me see her."

"I've already told you that my Pilar will be taking care of her. Besides, she can't testify against me now, can she? Once you're out of the way she'll go on with her life and you'll simply disappear from her memory."

John jumped out of his truck at the gate nearest to the harbor and took off running. He charged through a small group of people crossing in front of him, tripped over a man, and they both fell to the ground. The irate young man spewed expletives that had mothers covering their children's ears. John scrambled to his feet and kept running, skimming over the mass of people for any sign of Alex.

"John!"

He turned to see his stepfather pressing toward him. "Where is she, Hank?"

"I don't know. I saw her going toward the boardwalk and then I lost her. She could be anywhere."

John and Hank continued to push through. Suddenly John spotted her and pointed. "Over there."

"She's not alone."

"It's Rivera." John checked his weapon.

"John, you can't just start shootin' up the place."

John didn't respond. He forged ahead without excuses. Hank followed.

Fully expecting to die if she got into that car Alex knew she had to do something. If there was any hope at all of getting to Cerena, fight or flight were her only options. She pretended to lose her footing. Lurching forward she spun around and kneed Xavier in the groin. He yelped and doubled over. She kicked him again as hard as she could. He fell backward and she grabbed the gun.

In the distance Donovan emerged from the driver's side of the sedan just as John rounded the back side of the pizzeria. Donovan drew his weapon and took aim.

"Gun," shouted a passerby.

Horrified screams erupted. Those nearest to them panicked and separated, ducking for cover as Donovan squeezed the trigger and hit John squarely in the chest. Alex turned to look in the direction of the blast and saw John as he staggered to the pavement. She didn't have enough time to react before Xavier regained his equilibrium and leapt toward her. Knocking her to the ground they rolled around and wrestled for his gun. It went off and shot a woman in the leg who was cowering a few feet away. Xavier punched Alex in the face. The gun discharged again.

Pandemonium exploded. Milton Toliver and several security police charged through the mob, brandishing their own weapons.

"Drop it, Donovan," Toliver yelled. "Get down on your knees!"

Donovan slowly turned toward Toliver and started to lower the gun, but in a kneejerk move he fired on him. The shot missed and lodged in a wooden sign over his head. Reacting quickly Toliver fired his weapon twice. The first shot hit Donovan in his left arm. The second fatal shot hit him in the head.

Alex shifted uneasily under the weight of Rivera's body. One of the officers helped her to her feet and she broke away from him and ran over to where John lay.

"Stay with me, son," Hank cried, cradling John's head. "You got way too much to live for. You need to think about John Michael and Chloe and . . ."

Alex clasped her hand across her mouth and slowly knelt on the other side of the two. John opened his eyes and reached for her. Tears flowed down the side of his face and blood trickled from the corners of his mouth.

"I told you, I haven't . . . lost anybody I was assigned . . . to protect," he choked.

Alex cried. "You can't leave me."

John reached up and caressed Alex's face. Each breath was a struggle. You could literally hear the gurgle of blood filling up in his lungs. "I . . . wanted to tell you that . . . I . . . love . . ."

She took his hand and kissed it. "I love you," she whispered.

The faint sound of sirens in the distance grew louder as they got closer. People stood around gawking, some were crying, all were comforting one another.

John turned to Hank. "You need to tell Mama . . . " His eyes fluttered and then he was gone.

Alex heaved as tears of anguish rolled down her cheeks and pooled at the base of her neck. She lowered her face and gently kissed John's lips.

The perimeter of the ghastly scene was cordoned off and the crowd was swiftly ushered away from the vicinity of the boardwalk and out of the park as John, Xavier, and Donovan's bodies were removed. A search of the car turned up evidence that would lead them to the Four Seasons.

22

Pilar was stunned by the breaking news she watched unfold on television. The extent of devastation at the pier was astounding. There was no contingency plan discussed should Xavier's plot fail to yield the desired results. "*¡Dios mío!*" Frenetic energy coursed through her as she paced the floor ferociously, pulling her fingers through her silky raven mane. With the plan to drive across the US border into Mexico now defunct she needed to act quickly. Picking up the short blond wig that was purchased for her disguise she frantically tucked her hair underneath it. "*Esto es absolutamente una locura!*"

After checking herself in a mirror she scrambled around the hotel suite, collecting her passport and nearly $10,000 cash that Xavier had left behind. She then called for a car, threw some things into a bag for her and the baby, and bolted for the door. Cerena's unabated cries informed Pilar that she would not be pacified. "*Tenga en una pequeña y tranquila. Tu mamá está aquí.*"

Donning a large pair of dark sunglasses she stepped onto the elevator, rocking and shushing Cerena. The few others already on cleared their throats and shot her irritated side-glances. When the doors opened the concierge nodded toward Pilar and a female marshal rushed toward her.

"Pilar Vélez?"

Pilar continued through the lobby as if she didn't hear. Cerena's cries grew louder. Milton Toliver approached and grabbed her by the arm. Her bag fell to the floor and clothes and money scattered. The female marshal took hold of Cerena as another officer hurried to assist in Pilar's capture.

Toliver snatched off her wig and glasses to assure a positive identification. "Pilar Vélez, you're under arrest for kidnapping, murder, and conspiracy to commit murder."

Hotel guests and staff clustered, pointed, and stared.

Pilar thrashed around to free herself. "*Cabrón,* let go of me. I didn't do nothing."

"I wouldn't exactly call murder and kidnapping nothing," Toliver sniped as he twisted her wrists into handcuffs.

"*¡Eres un hijo de puta! Quítame las manos de encima!*"

"Blah, blah, blah. Yada, yada, yada," Toliver snarled. "I would exercise the right to remain silent if I were you." He dragged her to a waiting car and shoved her inside.

Having cleaned up the blood from her face and hands and given an unflattering change of clothes, Alex bolted from another car as the agent emerged from inside the lobby of the Four Seasons with Cerena. The agent handed the baby to Alex and she held her tightly, smothering her with kisses and tears.

"We have to go now," Toliver said as he ushered Alex into his car.

Alex breathed a sigh of relief. "I can't wait to see my mother."

"You'll see your mother soon enough. You've got a statement to give and I've got a lot of questions that need answers."

Alex shook her head. "I can't deal with any of that right now."

"You don't have a choice," Toliver snapped.

Alex steeled herself and glared back at him. "Choice is the one thing that you're not going to take from me. I'm not answering any of your questions until I see my mother."

Convinced that Alex would not relent, Inspector Toliver backed off and whisked her away to the undisclosed safe house where Jamilah was being kept. When they arrived he checked the security detail and pulled Alex to the side. "They'll be an armed guard outside your door tonight and a patrol outside the building. I'll be back here first thing in the morning, at which time I expect you to choose to cooperate."

Jamilah and Alex's reunion was bittersweet. They clung to one another and cried.

"It's over, Mama."

"Thank God you and Cerena are safe. I was beginning to think . . . Never mind; it doesn't matter now. What's important is that you're here and we're all together again."

Alex broke from Jamilah's embrace, laid Cerena down on a bed that was in the room, and sobbed more vehemently.

"What is it, Omolola?" She noted the bruises on her face. "What happened?"

Alex gently rubbed her cheek. "It's nothing. I'm okay."

"Inspector Chase? Where is he?"

Alex wailed and covered her mouth to keep from disturbing Cerena, who'd drifted to sleep. She shook her head in disbelief. "John is dead."

Jamilah gasped and clutched her chest. "What? How did this happen?"

"It was Harley Donovan. He was working with Xavier Rivera all this time."

"Oh, dear God. How did you find this out?"

"It's a long story, one that I can't get into right now."

"What about Xavier Rivera? Did they catch him?"

Alex hesitated and wiped her tears. She turned to Jamilah. "He's dead too. I shot him."

"Alexandra."

"Everything happened so fast. There were people and guns and chaos. It was horrible. Now John is dead and it's all my fault."

Jamilah took Alex in her arms. "No, Omolola. You can't blame yourself."

"I loved him, Mama. Now he's gone," she cried.

Jamilah's heart broke for her daughter. There were no words to ease her pain. She had to feel the loss and process it in her own way and in her own time.

23

Nearly a week had gone by since John's death. Once she gave her statement, with Xavier Rivera out of the picture, Alex felt that there was no longer a need for her to be part of the WITSEC program and requested to leave it. She understood that getting out meant she'd no longer be protected nor would she be allowed back in. She informed Chief Inspector Toliver of her intent to return to Nigeria with her mother and daughter. Under the circumstances he agreed to comply and began the necessary paperwork and the arduous process to release them.

Reports of the bloody skirmish on the Santa Monica Pier continued to dominate the news outlets. There was widespread conjecture surrounding all that had transpired, but a tight lid was kept on everything having to do with Alex Solomon and her involvement. Unfortunately the high profile of a man like Xavier Rivera was not so easily reined in. News of his demise ran wild. A report of the death of John Chase was a small but significant footnote to this story, as he was credited for tracking Rivera down and bringing him to a decisive and final end.

When Alex heard where John's memorial was being held she knew she had to be there. Jamilah objected. "Omolola, do you think that is wise given everything that's happened?"

"It's because of everything that's happened that I have to be there, Mama."

"Then I'll go with you."

"No, you stay with Cerena. I have to do this alone."

It seemed an ominous cloud hung over Mount Paran
Baptist Church in Inglewood despite the warmth of June.
There had been a constant flow of traffic all morning of
those coming to pay tribute to the life of a fallen hero. A
dark hearse with small American flags waving from either
side of the hood was anchored outside the church. There
was a line of cars behind it also standing ready to attend
to the bereaved family once the service concluded.

Inside the sanctuary over a hundred mourners had
gathered and sat solemnly as the organist played a litany
of music Barbara Mitchell had selected that would honor
her son's life the most. John was never the churchgoer
that his mother was. But on those rare occasions, when
she insisted, he was there sitting right beside her, clap-
ping and singing as if he'd always been there. She sat
in the front pew, staring directly at the open casket that
held John's lifeless body. Hank sat on one side of her and
her eldest son, Anthony, sat on the other. Their shared
sorrow eased the tension between Barbara and her
inconsolable daughter-in-law Lorraine, who sat on the
opposite side of Hank with Chloe on her lap and holding
on to John Michael's hand. Lorraine's parents, Liam
and Madeline, sat behind them. Milton Toliver, Sam
McFarland, and several police officers and marshals were
also in attendance.

Alex stepped into the sanctuary and almost immediately drew inquisitive whispers and accusatory stares.
The gossip that John and Lorraine's rumored separation
was careening toward divorce court and that there was
another woman involved was now verified with her presence. Despite concerted efforts at understated glamour,

with her hair pulled back and dressed in a simple form-
fitting sleeveless black dress, Alex still found herself to
be a ready target. She stopped and glared back at those
nearest the door and took a few moments to gather
herself. Swallowing apprehension she continued up the
aisle toward the casket to say a final good-bye.

Barbara Mitchell turned around when the disruption
reached her ear. She knew from everything Hank was
finally able to tell her that this was the woman at the
heart of all of her anguish. Letting go of Hank's hand
she stood up slowly. He tried to grab her arm and she
yanked it away. All eyes watched her as she stepped into
the aisle and stopped Alex in her tracks. Hank stood up
behind her. Barbara's tear-stained eyes and grief-stricken
expression raised the curtain on her years.

"Mrs. Mitchell, I'm so—"

Before Alex could complete her condolence Barbara
slapped her so hard across the face it caused her to lose
her footing and stumble a bit. Hank pulled his wife back
and Anthony rushed to assist.

"You're the reason he's dead! My son . . . my baby boy,"
Barbara cried. "You're not welcome here."

"Mrs. Mitchell, I—"

Barbara lost all decorum and began screaming. "Get
out! Get out! Get out!"

Alex looked to Hank as if he would somehow come to
her defense. He shook his head. Alex trembled as she
caught sight of Lorraine and Chloe and John Michael and
knew that her decision to come here had been a terrible
mistake. She backed up a few steps before turning and
running out of the church.

She ran up the block until she happened on a bus stop
and took a seat on a bench. Catching her breath and
drying her eyes she recalled the grieving faces of John's
children. Even though she knew of them somehow they

hadn't seemed real until now; their loss, their pain, was palpable.

Busses came and went. Passengers boarded and she sat. Finally, she spied the headlights of the hearse being escorted up the street by a platoon of motorcycle police. For fear of being seen she scurried behind a tree as the motorcade of cars passed. As the processional wound down she hailed a taxi and followed them to the cemetery. The mood at the cemetery was as somber as that in the church. Alex asked the cab driver to wait a safe distance away from the others as she witnessed the ritual of the last rites and the lowering of John's casket into the ground. Her pain, her tears, were no less ardent.

After a few minutes she instructed the driver to take her to the bank in Monrovia where she had her safety deposit box. It was almost an hour's drive, but it gave Alex enough time to decide what she had to do next.

She sat staring at the contents of a manila envelope: a letter to Tirrell Ellis, pictures of Cerena. Racked with guilt, she thought about all the children who may have lost fathers because of her dealings in Atlanta, and John Michael and Chloe, who'd lost their father when he was trying to protect her. Given what she'd caused to happen to Tirrell and his family, maybe she could be absolved of her sins in some small way if he were to know about Cerena. Pulling the letter out and tearing it up she put the pictures back inside the envelope and sealed it. She crossed out Betty Ellis's name and addressed it directly to Tirrell.

By the time she made it back to the tiny apartment she and Jamilah had transitioned to the day was well spent. The old was giving way to the new. A fresh start was on the horizon. Alex walked into the apartment, kicked off her shoes, and sat facing the window staring out at the orange, yellow, and crimson hues of a summer sunset. The view above the San Gabriel Mountains was nothing short of breathtaking, but all Alex could think about was another love lost.

"There you are," Jamilah said, coming in from the bedroom. "I was beginning to worry."

"I'm sorry, Mama. I had some things to take care of and time got away from me."

"How was the service?"

Alex smiled sadly. "I wouldn't know. John's mother was so angry with me she kicked me out of the church."

"Omolola, I wish you would have allowed me to go along with you."

"It wouldn't have made any difference. The end result would have most likely been the same."

"The service was at eleven," Jamilah noted. "It's almost seven. Where have you been all this time?"

"Believe it or not I went to the cemetery."

"Why torture yourself, daughter?"

"I had to say good-bye. Then I drove around in the cab and did some thinking. It felt so strange being out in the open for the first time and not being afraid."

Jamilah sat down in a chair facing Alex. "I for one can hardly wait to leave this godforsaken mess behind us. You are going to love Nigeria."

Alex sighed. "That's one of the things I was thinking about. Now that Xavier is dead and we're leaving the program nobody's chasing us anymore. We don't have any reason to run."

"You want to stay here in California?"

"Not necessarily. There are a couple of other places we could go. I think I've paid enough. Maybe God will give me a break now."

Jamilah stood, leaned into Alex, and kissed her fore-head. "Maybe you should give yourself a break, daughter."

"Where's Cerena?"

"I fed her and she's asleep. Can I fix you something to eat?"

"I'm not hungry."

Alex pushed herself up from the sofa and went to the room where Cerena slept. She tiptoed inside and watched her. "I did something today that I can't tell your *nnenne*. I don't know whether I should have or not, but it's done now. I sent your father pictures of you; I just hope I don't live to regret it." Alex's eyes misted. "*L'abe igi orombo . . . N'ibe . . . N'ibe . . .* "

Jamilah stepped up behind Alex, wrapped her arms around her and joined her in the song. "*N'ibe l'agbe nsere wa . . . Inu wa dun, ara wa ya . . . L'abe igi orombo . . . Orombo, orombo . . . Orombo, orombo.*"

Alex leaned in and kissed Cerena. "Sleep tight, my angel."

Despite all that remained from the wreckage of the past months it was a strangely peaceful moment. It was as close to normal as most anything else.

Epilogue

The Eastland Avenue neighborhood seemed more quiet than usual. Tirrell Ellis emerged from the brick-front house he still shared with his grandmother to retrieve the mail. Because of the brutal attack he'd suffered two years prior he now had to walk with a cane and the limp favoring his left side. He nodded to a neighbor across the street who was also checking her mail. The box was filled with grocery store coupons and bills, but a manila envelope addressed to him caught his attention.

He hobbled back into the house and laid the bulk of the mail on the dining room table. He eased himself down into a chair and before opening the envelope he held it up to the light to see if he could tell what it contained. When he opened it, four pictures fell out onto the table. He stared intently at the images of the baby girl in the photographs whose hazel eyes were the reflection of his own. He turned one over. All that was there was the name Cerena and the date May 15, 2009. For some inexplicable reason he felt a tug that he hadn't expected. He checked the envelope for a return address and read the postmark from Monrovia, California. He leaned back in his chair, staring at the baby, rubbed his hand over his faded haircut and whispered, "Alex."

"Tirrell, are you all right?"

Tirrell looked up to see that his grandmother Betty had come in from the kitchen. "Uh, I don't exactly know what I am right now, Noonie."

"What's the matter?"

Tirrell handed her the pictures. She wiped her hands on the towel she carried, sat down in a chair beside him, and carefully examined the images. "Cerena," she said aloud. "Whose child is this?"

"Who does she look like to you?" he asked.

The stout woman pulled on her reading glasses and thoughtfully rubbed her fingers over her lips and then traced the outline of the photograph. "She looks like you when you were a baby."

"Congratulations, Noonie. I think you're a great-grandmother, again."

"What?" The woman's stunned expression spoke volumes. "Tirrell, where did these pictures come from?"

"They came in the mail," he responded. "In this envelope. It has a postmark from California."

"California?"

"I think Alex Solomon sent them. I think that girl is my daughter."

"Oh, Tirrell, what would make you say such a thing?"

Tirrell leaned intently toward his grandmother. "Don't you see, Noonie? Alex made a deal with the Feds and got ghost. Two weeks ago we hear on the news that Xavier Rivera is dead. Now all of a sudden I get this in the mail. If it's not from her, who could it be from then?"

Betty Ellis removed her glasses, shook her head, and closed her eyes. Tirrell awkwardly pulled his lean six foot one inch frame up from the table and limped to the kitchen without his cane.

"Tirrell, what are you doing?"

"I'm gonna call Kevin. He's a DA. If Alex Solomon is alive and if that girl is mine then I need to find her."

"No, Tirrell," Betty admonished.

"What do you mean no? If Alex sent me those pictures she did it for a reason."

Betty stood up from the table, pressed her hands together, and walked over to him. "That woman was nothin' but trouble from the day you met her. For all you know this could all be some kind of hoax or scheme to get back at you."

Tirrell scoffed. "Get back at me for what, Noonie? I ain't got nothin' left that she wants."

Betty lovingly cupped her grandson's face in her hands. "Baby, after all the hell that woman put this family through you can't hope to find her and bring her back into our lives."

Tirrell pulled away. "I don't give a damn about Alex Solomon," he snapped. "If that girl is my daughter I have a right to know. And, if Alex gets in my way I'm gonna do what I should have done two years ago."

"Tirrell—"

"I mean it, Noonie! I'll kill her! This time, I swear to God. I'll kill her!"

ORDER FORM
URBAN BOOKS, LLC
97 N18th Street
Wyandanch, NY 11798

Name (please print):_____

Address: _____

City/State: _____

Zip: _____

QTY	TITLES	PRICE

Shipping and handling-add $3.50 for 1st book, then $1.75 for each additional book.

Please send a check payable to:

Urban Books, LLC

Please allow 4-6 weeks for delivery

ORDER FORM
URBAN BOOKS, LLC
97 N18th Street
Wyandanch, NY 11798

Name (please print):_____

Address: _____

City/State: _____

Zip: _____

QTY	TITLES	PRICE
	16 On The Block	$14.95
	A Girl From Flint	$14.95
	A Pimp's Life	$14.95
	Baltimore Chronicles	$14.95
	Baltimore Chronicles 2	$14.95
	Betrayal	$14.95
	Black Diamond	$14.95
	Black Diamond 2	$14.95
	Black Friday	$14.95
	Both Sides Of The Fence	$14.95
	Both Sides Of The Fence 2	$14.95
	California Connection	$14.95

Shipping and handling-add $3.50 for 1st book, then $1.75 for each additional book.

Please send a check payable to:
    Urban Books, LLC
Please allow 4-6 weeks for delivery

ORDER FORM
URBAN BOOKS, LLC
97 N18th Street
Wyandanch, NY 11798

Name (please print):_____

Address: _____

City/State: _____

Zip: _____

QTY	TITLES	PRICE
	California Connection 2	$14.95
	Cheesecake And Teardrops	$14.95
	Congratulations	$14.95
	Crazy In Love	$14.95
	Cyber Case	$14.95
	Denim Diaries	$14.95
	Diary Of A Mad First Lady	$14.95
	Diary Of A Stalker	$14.95
	Diary Of A Street Diva	$14.95
	Diary Of A Young Girl	$14.95
	Dirty Money	$14.95
	Dirty To The Grave	$14.95

Shipping and handling-add $3.50 for 1st book, then $1.75 for each additional book.
Please send a check payable to:
    Urban Books, LLC
Please allow 4-6 weeks for delivery

ORDER FORM
URBAN BOOKS, LLC
97 N18th Street
Wyandanch, NY 11798

Name (please print):_____

Address: _____

City/State: _____

Zip: _____

QTY	TITLES	PRICE
	Gunz And Roses	$14.95
	Happily Ever Now	$14.95
	Hell Has No Fury	$14.95
	Hush	$14.95
	If It Isn't love	$14.95
	Kiss Kiss Bang Bang	$14.95
	Last Breath	$14.95
	Little Black Girl Lost	$14.95
	Little Black Girl Lost 2	$14.95
	Little Black Girl Lost 3	$14.95
	Little Black Girl Lost 4	$14.95
	Little Black Girl Lost 5	$14.95

Shipping and handling-add $3.50 for 1st book, then $1.75 for each additional book.
Please send a check payable to:
Urban Books, LLC
Please allow 4-6 weeks for delivery

ORDER FORM
URBAN BOOKS, LLC
97 N18th Street
Wyandanch, NY 11798

Name (please print):_____

Address: _____

City/State: _____

Zip: _____

QTY	TITLES	PRICE
	Loving Dasia	$14.95
	Material Girl	$14.95
	Moth To A Flame	$14.95
	Mr. High Maintenance	$14.95
	My Little Secret	$14.95
	Naughty	$14.95
	Naughty 2	$14.95
	Naughty 3	$14.95
	Queen Bee	$14.95
	Say It Ain't So	$14.95
	Snapped	$14.95
	Snow White	$14.95

Shipping and handling-add $3.50 for 1st book, then $1.75 for each additional book.
Please send a check payable to:
Urban Books, LLC
Please allow 4-6 weeks for delivery

ORDER FORM
URBAN BOOKS, LLC
97 N18th Street
Wyandanch, NY 11798

Name (please print):_____

Address: _____

City/State: _____

Zip: _____

QTY	TITLES	PRICE
	Spoil Rotten	$14.95
	Supreme Clientele	$14.95
	The Cartel	$14.95
	The Cartel 2	$14.95
	The Cartel 3	$14.95
	The Dopefiend	$14.95
	The Dopeman Wife	$14.95
	The Prada Plan	$14.95
	The Prada Plan 2	$14.95
	Where There Is Smoke	$14.95
	Where There Is Smoke 2	$14.95

Shipping and handling-add $3.50 for 1st book, then $1.75 for each additional book.
Please send a check payable to:
Urban Books, LLC
Please allow 4-6 weeks for delivery

ORDER FORM
URBAN BOOKS, LLC
97 N18th Street
Wyandanch, NY 11798

Name (please print):_____

Address: _____

City/State: _____

Zip: ,   _____

QTY	TITLES	PRICE

Shipping and handling-add $3.50 for 1st book, then $1.75 for each additional book.

Please send a check payable to:

Urban Books, LLC

Please allow 4-6 weeks for delivery